ECHOES OF THE LONG WAR

THE BEAST ARISES

Discover the latest books in this multi-volume series at
blacklibrary.com

THE BEAST ARISES

BOOK SIX

ECHOES OF THE LONG WAR

DAVID GUYMER

BLACK LIBRARY

A BLACK LIBRARY PUBLICATION

First published in Great Britain in 2016 by
Black Library
Games Workshop Ltd
Willow Road
Nottingham NG7 2WS UK

10 9 8 7 6 5 4 3 2 1

Produced by Games Workshop in Nottingham

Fire sputters...
The shame of our deaths
and our heresies is done. They are
behind us, like wretched phantoms. This
is a new age, a strong age, an age of Imperium.
Despite our losses, despite the fallen sons, despite the
eternal silence of the Emperor, now watching over us in
spirit instead of in person, we will endure. There will be no
more war on such a perilous scale. There will be an end
to wanton destruction. Yes, foes will come and
enemies will arise. Our security will be
threatened, but we will be ready, our
mighty fists raised. There will be no
great war to challenge us now.
We will not be brought
to the brink like that
again...

To learn without thinking is dull, to think without learning is dangerous.

– from the teachings of the Ancient Confucian

ONE

Combat lighting cut uneven diagonal strokes across the command deck of the Fists Exemplar battle-barge *Dantalion*. She creaked and groaned like a submersible descending into the deep, uncharted black. The real space cocoon of her Geller field rippled under the eddying pressures of the empyrean.

From null-shielded podia positioned around the principal deck to form an apotropaic symbol, cherubic serfs of the Chapter Librarius sang warp-soothing verses. The vaulted, cathedral-like space had been designed as much for its acoustics as for its strategic value, for indeed what were the choristers but another aspect of defence? Within hermetically walled-off command turrets, operations serfs worked efficiently under grainy pools of light. Shotgun-wielding Chapter armsmen, in grey carapace armour devoid of insignia, watched over their bodies. The chorus soothed their doubts and girded their souls. Reinforced by the confessional susurrus of muted conversation and the continual lifting up and setting down of hardline communication units, the song echoed down the mighty support pillars to the cogitation tiers below. Mindless though they were, even the servitors and the clicking, whirring, humming machine-spirits they tended had their contribution to make to the chorale.

The refraction field that blanketed the blast doors powered down, and the metre-thick, silver-rebarred adamantium parted with a pneumatic hiss. A dozen multilaser cradles and frag-launchers pivoted to cover the kill-zone that ramped upwards from the doors to the deck.

That was the sum of the reaction generated by First Captain Zerberyn's arrival on deck. Fortunate then that he felt no need for the acclaim that Koorland and Thane received from the masses.

Zerberyn was humble, considered, austere: an Exemplar in his founder's example.

Deactivating the priority summons, he stamped up the ramp with a whine of actuators and power servos, a pale-faced giant encased in armour of unpainted grey ceramite. He was pale, because he was the mortal child of a world whose light could kill. He was a giant, because his gene-fathers had seen the worth of making him so.

He ascended the deck at the same time as the blast doors resealed and the refraction field snapped back to full power. He felt the auto-turrets disengage their lock on him and return to sentry protocols.

'Report, shipmaster.'

The crippled shipmaster stood stiffly in the middle of a ring of terminals in the vox-turret. His posture was no affectation. The augmetic brace that clad his entire right side in a metal skeleton and allowed him to stand did not also allow him to bend. He worked at attention, he ate at attention, he slept at attention. He glanced at the analogue chrono face mounted on the turret wall. It read 05:17. Still on Terran time.

'I hadn't expected you so soon.'

'Your summons was flagged "priority".'

As if to protest, Shipmaster Marcarian opened the corner of his mouth that still functioned, an eyelid flickering withlocked-in frustration, and stumped forty degrees about to face the vox-liaison. She was identically outfitted to the serfs she spoke for: glittering void suit, bulky headset, sidearm clamped under the rest of an armoured console chair. There was nothing to differentiate rank. Not on a Fists Exemplar ship.

The shipmaster worked saliva through his palsied mouth. '05:07, ship time, Vox logged receipt of an Adeptus Astartes distress beacon. Lexicography haven't yet purified enough of the signal corruption to retrieve the message.'

'The Navy abandons systems wholesale at the rumour of an attack moon in a neighbouring sector. Worlds burn, our own amongst them, the Throneworld itself is besieged, and hourly we receive a plea for deliverance. And you summon me for a distress beacon?'

'I trust you weren't called away from anything too pressing?'

Zerberyn looked down over the blinking lights of his gorget softseal.

Marcarian swallowed with difficulty. 'Just curious.'

'I was in the Locutory with Brother Columba. The sergeant and I were debating the meanings of Guilliman's extended proverbs.'

The shipmaster produced a smile. 'I've not yet had the chance to congratulate you on your promotion to captaincy of the First. The command crew held a vigil in your honour.'

'I chose not to attend.'

'Vardy brought amasec.' Marcarian's good eye wandered towards the spiralling waves on the vox-liaison's screen. 'We were able to provision a crate on Terra. The lord sergeant would be a worthy First Captain, but he's a hard... task... master...'

Zerberyn's eyes drilled parallel holes into the side of the shipmaster's head. The man cleared his throat.

'We have something,' said the vox-liaison, crisply.

'Go ahead,' Marcarian breathed. 'Please.'

'It's definitely Last Wall.'

It would have taken one even more attuned to Space Marine physiology than the two mortal crew members to note the tightening muscles of Zerberyn's neck. The Last Wall was an abhorrence to him. The mere conception of it would have been affront enough to Guilliman's legacy, and that it was *his own primarch* that had done so sickened him. It had been Oriax Dantalion himself, the visionary who would later found the Fists Exemplar, who had persuaded Dorn of the wisdom in Guilliman's solution. And now the Fists Exemplar had discovered that the primarch was not persuaded after all.

Zerberyn had argued the case with Thane at Phall, as he knew Dantalion himself would have done had he still lived, and had done so again on Terra. Another might have viewed his subsequent elevation in spite of all that had gone before as evidence of Thane's magnanimity, but Zerberyn knew him better. It was an insult. The First had already been culled of its finest to reform Koorland's shield corps. He was captain of the First, but the First was a company of new recruits and stubborn ideologues like Columba, who would rather lay down their arms and let destruction find them than don the black fist of Dorn once more.

'What does it say?'

'I wouldn't advise listening to it. There's a verbal component but it's been heavily corrupted by the transition to the empyreal phase. But I do have coordinates.'

'Is it Phall? I told Thane that Koorland was premature to depart while the Soul Drinkers and the bulk of the Black Templars were still to be contacted.'

The vox-liaison shook her head. 'No. The latest navigation estimate puts us at least several weeks from the rendezvous coordinates. It's not Terra either.' She pivoted her chair and called up a screed of data to her terminal. Gloved fingers dancing over the keys, she transformed it into what Zerberyn recognised as a four-dimensional coordinate plot. 'It's close by, originating from an orphan star in the Sycrax Cluster. A red giant called Vandis.'

'Is Thane or anyone else receiving this beacon?'

The officer sucked in her teeth, frustrated as much with herself as with the difficulties imposed on her by warp physics. 'I don't know.'

Zerberyn looked up to where the main viewscreen hung suspended from a plasteel gantry, reassuringly blank save for a purity seal on a fuzzy grey background. It was blustery with static, interpretive in its not-quite-random swirls of the buffeting energies of the warp.

With superhuman speed of thought, he collated the available variables, assembling them into a plan of action that he then challenged with every conceivable scenario. He took the additional half-second required to satisfy himself that any ship in the Fists Exemplar fleet in possession of the same information would reach an identical conclusion.

He had no love for his distant gene-brothers, but like it or not they were the Last Wall. The Imperium stood only while they held firm, and as the Arch-Heretic himself had annihilated the last great ork empire at its root, so too would Zerberyn burn the Beast from the very ground on which he lived.

This, he promised to himself.

'Contact the *Alcazar Remembered* or any other ship you can raise, and transmit a data-burst containing the beacon coordinates and our course of action.'

'Which is?' said Marcarian.

'Prepare for immediate real space translation onto the origin of that beacon. All stations to battle readiness. All weapons systems and shield arrays to be engaged the second we emerge.'

The shipmaster nodded stiffly and began to relay orders to the relevant stations, which in turn disseminated them through the ship down their hardlines. The murmur of voices became a clamour.

'To run blind into a battle is folly,' Marcarian murmured, for Zerberyn's ear alone.

'I know well the lessons of the *Codex Astartes*, shipmaster.'

Marcarian bowed his head. 'Let me at least recommend that *Excelsior* be sent in ahead. She's Rubicante-class, designed to operate through the worst distortions of the Flux. Her vox-array should be more than powerful enough to reach us, even here.'

Zerberyn duly considered the shipmaster's counter-proposal. Coordinating the actions of a fleet the size of the Fists Exemplar's through the immaterium would be fraught at best. Who could say what was listening? Or worse, what truly answered. He could not even say with certainty where *Excelsior* or the *Alcazar Remembered* were, or that they had not already emerged into the materium at Phall.

It was possible that *Dantalion* would return to Phall in a month's time and find that *Excelsior* and the rest of the fleet had never left.

Zerberyn's thumb rolled over his bolt pistol's holster lock. It was Umbra-pattern, lacking the refinement of post-Heresy models, the various augmentations and integrations that had come with subsequent improvements in power armour design, but it was good at what it was made for and always would be. Purity through utility: that was how one proofed oneself against the unknowables of the galaxy.

He made his decision.

Guilliman's writings spoke often of the importance of recognising the least worst option and seizing it.

'Take us in.'

Vandis System – Mandeville point

Zerberyn felt a squeeze on his brain as though something were trying to get in. He heard whispers, and ignored them.

He saw things – things he could not ignore so easily. He saw Dantalion.

Zerberyn was a relative neophyte, a recruit of the Chapter's Eidolican era. He had never seen Oriax Dantalion, but he knew with the conviction of his genetics that it was him. Zerberyn did not speak, nor was he spoken to, but just watched as Sigismund, Alexis Polux, Demetrius Katafalque, and then Rogal Dorn himself turned their backs on the first Exemplar one by one. Zerberyn felt anger, but he was helpless to express it to these titanic figures. Without appearing to transition, Dantalion's armour had ceased to be gold, but it had not become the unvarnished grey of Zerberyn's own.

It was gunmetal and bronze.

Translation was complete, but this part was the worst. Those few seconds after the warp drives had powered down and the Geller field had collapsed, but the empyreal sheath remained raw and unhealed, thin enough to touch the other side with one's mind, and for the waking nightmares that dwelled there to, if only for a few seconds, touch back.

The vision faded as the materium resealed, and Zerberyn dwelled on its lies no further.

Klaxons screamed proximity alerts and a dozen different types of weapons lock. Alert runes cycled amber and red. Their warnings went unheeded for a few critical seconds more, the unimproved brain chemistries of *Dantalion*'s mortal crew requiring that extra time to recover from the ordeal of translation.

Zerberyn killed an automated low-shield sounder with a gauntlet-mash that deactivated several other warning icons and cracked the terminal.

'Steady as she goes,' Marcarian drooled, straight as a cane, stiffened by his augmetic brace and implant while those around were still slumped with harrowed expressions in their chairs. 'Cycle plasma coils. Navigational shields to full power. Void shield generators to cover all quadrants. Weapon grids online. Full spectrum sweep and re-initialise main viewer. Someone find me the source of that distress beacon.'

A dulled chorus of 'Aye, sirs' answered him. A string of light impacts trembled through the massive vessel's hull as the main viewscreen wiped its purity seal and shivered online. It was a default forward shot: the gothic grey armour of *Dantalion*'s prow. A squadron of supercharged ork fighter-bombers streaked across it, trailed by a line of explosions.

'Shields,' said Zerberyn.

'Void banks to charge in three... two... one.'

A resonant harmonic thrummed over the systems' noise and the cherub-serfs' chorus. The fighter-bomber to the rear of the orks' chaotic formation was swallowed up by a ball of fire as *Dantalion*'s port-forward void shield manifested within its fuselage and ripped the craft to pieces. A wave of static washed across the viewscreen. Zerberyn focused. His occulobe organ was designed for low-light conditions and hyperfine details, and it autonomically filtered the visual noise.

The murderous red glow of the stellar giant, Vandis, flooded the shot and robbed the void of stars. In their place, he saw explosions, propellant burns and a glittering shoal of red-lit predators. It was a void fight, and a major one. He counted at least two hundred ork cruisers, possibly more. Pre-translation inertia carried them towards the battle at several hundred kilometres per second.

'Ship contacts!' came the shout from the strategium, a second behind. The liaison serf there held an internal vox-horn to his ear.

'Ours?' said Marcarian.

'Too many!'

A flare lit the viewer, something massive-yield thumping the forward shield hard enough to shake the deck plates of the command bridge.

'Try to raise the rest of the fleet,' ordered Marcarian. 'If they haven't joined us then we don't stand a chance.'

'Aye, sir.'

'They will be here,' said Zerberyn. 'If even one ship received our transmission then they would have signalled also and the probability of a third vessel receiving would be doubled, and so on, exponentially. We are in the only place that any brother in receipt of those coordinates could be.'

'We should at least be prepared to withdraw. Permission to re-actuate warp drives and lock-down for an emergency translation.'

'Granted. Caution is always the wisest course when others fail to present themselves.'

'Very good, lord captain.' Marcarian stumped off to distribute orders.

'Find me that distress beacon, shipmaster.'

'Come and look at this, lord captain.'

Marcarian was standing by the chart desk that dominated the strategium turret. The base unit was an illuminated table, above which a wavering hololithic grid chart was displayed. A golden aquila dead-centre represented *Dantalion*. She was surrounded by a cloud of unidentified blips, trailing back towards the bloated, crimson wire-frame that represented the Vandis star. The intervening grids filled fast with ship markers, like a spreading infection reviewed on rapid playback. The banks of time-lapse and repeater screens that surrounded the desk were walled with static.

'Disregard the orks for now,' Marcarian commanded the strategium liaison. 'Authorise removal of the necessary coding wafers and route the spared cogitation capacity to parse Last Wall identifiers.'

'Do you not want targets?' asked Zerberyn.

'Scanning for Last Wall signals will identify both the source of the distress beacon, and our own fleet if they are here. That should be our first priority.'

Zerberyn offered his silence by way of agreement. Before a void fight with a Death Guard flotilla had wasted his right side and earned him his command, Marcarian had been Augur Master aboard the *Grey Ranger*. He knew his system.

'I'd also recommend mobilising the First. The orks have shown themselves to favour long-range teleport actions.'

It was then that Zerberyn realised that at some point during the translation cycle he had drawn his pistol.

'We are ready for them.'

All Adeptus Astartes fleets employed the same classes of ship, but the modular design allowed for variations on the basic STC. Fists Exemplar warships differed from those of their cousins in many ways, but principal among these was the manifold layers of dedicated psychic shielding they employed. They were built for void-war, purposed to patrol the storm-wracked region of wilderness space afflicted by the Rubicante Flux. In addition to the cherub-serfs that filled every inhabited section with song, choristers from the Chapter Librarius psychically conducted the chorus from chambers specifically designed for their warp-soothing acoustics. Every one of *Dantalion*'s millions of consoles was worked with monomolecular silver wires. Her ballast chambers were filled with the scent of candlewood and samphyr, silvic oil and rose cedar. Even the very halls of the ship were arranged into the schematised form of potent protective runes and a good portion of her orbit-to-ground firepower had been retrofitted with psychic null generators.

She had been designed to fight the enemies of Man and triumph in regions of space where other ships could not enter, and only deep-survey barges of the Inquisition sailed with greater protection against warp-borne assault.

'But again, granted. Have them deploy at your discretion.'

'Bright skies...' someone exclaimed.

Zerberyn followed the staring faces to the main viewscreen. Someone amongst the veteran crew zoomed the screen's visual feed and placed a bracket around a patched-up old colossus. Almost three times the mass of *Dantalion*, it looked like an Imperial Navy battleship. It was heavily damaged and, so it appeared, either partially or carelessly rebuilt. Its aft section was almost completely crumpled, and had been fitted with a monstrous engine housing almost as large as the rest of the ship that filled the void behind it with cones of chemical fire. Construction scaffolds spread from the hull like a beetle's wings. Fires burned on several decks.

'Oberon-class,' Marcarian confirmed. 'Or she was.'

The big vessel yawed into the lower quadrant of the main viewer, drifting across the plane of the solar system with a trail of gnat-like ork fighters in pursuit. 'Approaching on an intercept vector.'

Whatever their current naval supremacy, the orks would always make use of what they found. Zerberyn could almost respect them for that.

'No serial codes, no auto-transmissions, no response to hails.' Marcarian limped through the strategium desks, looking over shoulders at the read-outs. 'I'd say it's an ork ship.'

'Of course it is an ork ship. That much is clear.'

'Still no sign of Last Wall transponders on our scans, lord captain,' said Marcarian, stiffly. 'All hands ready for emergency translation at your order.'

Zerberyn brought the barrel of his pistol to his gorget ring and tapped it as he thought, watching the zipping ork fighters wind about the nearing battleship like surgical thread through a wound.

'Lord captain, I think that–'

'I commend you your unfettered thought, it improves us all,' Zerberyn spat, quoting from the *Oriax Variorum*. The ship slid into full view, *Dantalion* gunning for it amidships. Zerberyn aimed his bolt pistol at the viewer.

'Kill that ship.'

TWO

Terra – the Imperial Palace

The shuttle deployed its landing struts for its final descent stage onto Daylight Pad Theta, the light void craft wobbling in the crosswinds generated by the perpetual grind of the Palace hive's colossal cycler fans and the sheer volume of air traffic. Transorbital lighters were picking up and setting down in a near-constant flow, crowding the Palace's sky-line: red and purple and black and gold, a swirling plasteel snow of new conscripts pressed into the Navy's proudest regiments. To navigate a shuttle through either obstacle, let alone both, was a task closer to reading the Emperor's Tarot than landing a void craft. To even make the attempt took the superhuman reflexes and unshakable confidence of the Adeptus Astartes.

Koorland, Chapter Master of the Imperial Fists, looked up to watch the shuttle's approach.

Waves of promethium heat beat down on him, and the roar of the angling turbofans rippled his lips and cheeks, but his eyes stayed open despite the onslaught. The Templar crosses emblazoned on white panels on the shuttle's nose and underwing appeared to resize as aerofoils made minute adjustments. Jets of air from lateral stabilisation thrusters held it level. Roused from torpor by the approaching lander and flushed of soporific neurosedatives, servitors bonded to caterpillar-tracked motive assemblies moved haltingly forwards against the jetwash. Lengths of bright orange vulcanised hosing played out behind them, the oil-washed outlet valves supplanting superfluous hands and emerging from artificially gaping mouths flanked by mind-wiped stares.

The shuttle touched down within the innermost ring of blinking guidelights, and eased onto its landing struts. The roar of its turbofans became a whine and gases hissed from heat flues and radiator grilles, equalising pressure and temperature across the shuttle's glowing heat-shields. One of the servitor units sprayed the shuttle with super-cooled carbon dioxide vapour. Another trundled underneath, frozen gases crystallising its slack features, and nozzled its wrist adaptor over the shuttle's filler pipe. It emitted a guzzling noise, smoking under the white hiss of venting gases.

Either side of Koorland, an honour detail of human (and another of not-quite-human) troopers endeavoured to stand crisply at attention, despite the successive waves of engine heat and coolant that came at them from the middle of the pad.

The men were all tall and hard-faced, in black uniforms with red piping and frogging, armsmen of the Navy's symbolic flagship, the *Royal Barque*. Each wore the *Royal Barque*'s forbidding ensign on their shoulder in place of the usual regimental insignia, a sheathed cutlass and a pair of ceremonial red gloves. They were the Navy's elite protection detail, and only the highest-ranking admirals and most influential of visiting dignitaries warranted such bodyguards. In this instance, the subject of their care was Rear-Admiral Pervez Leshento of the Tiamat-class battleship *Dies Dominus*. The name was High Gothic for 'Lord of Daylight'. An extraordinary coincidence, or Lansung was honeying Koorland's gruel a little thickly.

On the other side were the skitarii of the Basilikon Astra, the exploratory fleets of Mars: visored, cloaked in dark, energy-dense robes worn over a bio-augmented flesh-carapace and an assortment of techno-esoterica. Koorland doubted that the cyborgised warriors suffered the extremes of heat and cold gushing out from the shuttle pad, but the jetwash was certainly fighting them over their heavy cloaks. The commander of the maniple was a magos explorator named Benzeine. He was wrapped up to his throat in deep red robes woven with the machina opus. From the odd, twitching motions that occasionally stirred these robes, they were to protect the sensibilities of those he moved amongst rather than for his own benefit. Hololithic equations hovered about a millimetre in front of his black-chrome facial dish from a miniaturised projector embedded somewhere amidst the array of fluttering sensors.

The Taghmata of Mars had fulfilled their obligations in the Last Wall's assault on the ork attack moon, limited though they were, and the Fabricator General was not about to relinquish control of that orbiting planetoid of xeno-tech now.

As Koorland waited, a pair of hypersonic Lightning interceptors rocketed overhead, the second surfing on its leader's contrail. An expanding, rolling boom rattled the ornamental flak turrets of Dawn Spire and the leaded windows of the Walk of Heroes on the other side of the killing ground. The golden vexillum of the Daylight militia that flew from the plasteel-plated turrets of the Cathedral of Saint Clementine the Absolver bent after the passing fighters. Koorland looked up to catch them but even his genhanced eyes were too slow.

Instead, distorted by stained plex-glass and cracked UV-shielding, he saw the ork moon. Its cratered face glared down through a tangle of piping as if it always knew exactly when and where to look to find him. It was far smaller than Terra's own moon, but hanging in geostationary orbit just a few hundred kilometres above the Sanctum Imperialis it appeared ten times larger. The larger vessels of the blockading fleet – *Autocephalax Eternal*, *Dies Dominus* and *Abhorrence* being but three – were visible from Terra, like clouds passing slowly over the face of the hostile alien planetoid. Koorland himself knew no fear, but despite the visual reassurance, he could well understand the terror the ork moon instilled in people.

Even those who would never see the sky could feel its power over their world.

A tremor passed through the mountainous bastion of Daylight Wall. Unsecured maintenance hatches rattled. Fern-like communications vanes hummed, the indelicate side-to-side motion transformed into harmonic vibrations. The mighty fortifications moved, as they had been designed to move under tectonic stresses or the crushing overpressure of an artillery bombardment, but their superficial facades crumbled, tank-sized chunks of ornamental masonry crashing down into the killing fields and the under-hives. Cabling tore – electrical, hydraulic, plasmic – and ionised gases and pressurised fluids sprayed photochemical ejecta into the Palace twilight.

The shaking eased. The shouts of rescue and repair units filtered up from below.

Things were not, at least, as dire as they had become on Ardamantua. The Last Wall and Basilikon Astra's bombardment had obliterated the attack moon's weaponry along with about ninety-five per cent of its crust. No, this was not a weapon. This was simply the seismic shock of having a lunar body suddenly transposed into near orbit.

He looked across the fretted robes of the skitarii, dazzling the air with arcane symbology, to where Daylight stood on the opposite side of the platform with his back against the steep drop to the Palace. The Fists Exemplar battle-brother who had taken the name, formerly Seventh Captain Dentor, looked good in his new livery, as much as it pained Koorland to compel his brother to wear it. He knew the value that the warrior's home Chapter placed on outward humility and inward pride. The golden spear and shield he carried were not the same as those borne by his namesake, for they too had been victims of Ardamantua's destruction, but had been selected for him from the Chapter's armouries on the basis of being a good enough likeness to fool anyone who was not a son of Dorn.

To his dishonour, it did feel good to share his wall with a

brother again. And Lord Udo had been right. The populace appreciated the sight of Imperial Fists on the walls.

Daylight nodded the all-clear, and Koorland returned it.

In a squeal of hydraulics, the shuttle's boarding hatch lowered. The ramp struck the platform with a dull metallic thump, flexing and rattling as if in the grip of another quake as the power-armoured High Marshal of the Black Templars emerged through the coolant vapours.

Bohemond's face was a burned ruin, scorched by the witch-fire of an ork psyker in a battle long before the present uprising. Half of what remained was a metal mask as emotive as the chrome plate of the magos explorator, but the other half was what struck terror into mortals and transhumans alike. It was flesh, but it could not be called a face. Looking at it, you could see where flesh had run, where it had resolidifed as he beat the greenskin witch to death with his bare fists, and the new form it had taken.

Koorland was not above a slight feeling of intimidation. Whatever he felt was amplified in the mortal soldiery tenfold. The idea that they might offer any protection at all against even the one Space Marine was laughable.

The High Marshal carried Sigismund's sword in one gauntleted fist, drawn, the long blade angled away from him and towards the ground. The other hand he presented, palm up, and waited for half a second while a warrior bondsman in bone-coloured flak armour and black surplice slapped a data-slate into it. It looked as though he was about to launch into some kind of prepared speech.

But Koorland had come to know him better than that.

'The last coordinates of every Black Templars, Crimson

Fists, Excoriators and Iron Knights ship in the blockade fleet, and the codes to our defensive installations in the base's interior.' Bohemond's mouth no longer closed properly and the expression he made was a loathsome sneer. 'I advise you to memorise them. By the High Lords' decree, there remain enough orks in the deeper levels to occupy your surface teams.'

Bohemond looked from Benzeine to Leshento, waving the slate back and forth in his giant's hand as though hoping the two men might fight each other to be the one to have it. Neither would have dared. With a scowl, the High Marshal tossed the slate dismissively into the hands of one of the *Royal Barque* soldiers.

The information could have been delivered by data-burst, but the wheels of Terran bureaucracy were greased by such petty ceremonies.

The skitarii and Navy men filed out. The single Adeptus Arbites enforcer guarding the steps down to the fifth tier battlements saluted the magos explorator and the rear-admiral. Koorland was uncertain what she was there for. He smiled slightly.

His protection, he presumed.

As the last of the men disappeared down the steps, Bohemond strode across the platform and clasped Koorland by the forearm. Koorland returned the pressure on the High Marshal's elbow guard.

'It is good to see a friendly face, brother.'

'Is that a joke?'

Koorland grunted, amused, but no longer seemed to feel like smiling. They released each other's arms and stepped

back, almost wary. 'You have not come around to Udo's edict, I take it,' Koorland said.

'If he wishes to disperse the Chapters, then I say let him try and make us.'

'Mind what you say, brother. Your anger at the High Lords' ingratitude is understandable. I share it. But it is because of thoughts like these that we must disperse.'

'I do not care about their ingratitude,' Bohemond muttered darkly. 'It is their ineptitude that concerns me.'

'If it will keep the Council on my side then having you and the others join the Fists Exemplar at Phall is a small price.'

'And if the orks simply lie in wait for such an opening? There could be millions yet in the attack moon's core, biding their time, and as the Mechanicus did not permit us to delve deeper we cannot say for certain that we destroyed the only teleportation device they have.'

'Phall is little more than a month away at worst, and fifty Space Marine veterans is no token force.'

To be counted amongst a Space Marine Chapter's finest was no small thing, and from the First Companies of the Fists Exemplar, Black Templars, Crimson Fists, Excoriators and Iron Knights, Koorland had reconstituted the shield corps. Daylight. Hemisphere. Tranquility. Bastion Ledge. Ballad Gate. Zarathustra. Lotus Gate. He meant no disrespect to the Lucifer Blacks, who had stepped up to fill the Imperial Fist-sized breach in Fortress Terra, but they were not Space Marines. War would undoubtedly come again to the Imperial Palace, and when it did, then like the Arch-Traitor before them, the orks would meet walls defended by the sons of Dorn.

'Can you hold for that long?' said Bohemond.

'It is ground, brother. I can hold it.'

Bohemond revealed his twisted grin, as if he were show-ing off a knife, and he nodded across Koorland's shoulder. The enforcer had approached and halted about two metres away and threw a salute.

'I know you, enforcer,' said Koorland.

The part of the woman's face that was visible between her chinstraps and visor seemed suddenly to glow. It was a look that Koorland had become wearily familiar with amongst the Palace's mortal defenders. The sort of look reserved for saints and saviours. 'Galatea Haas, lord, and,' she rolled her shoulder to show her rank stripes, 'it's proctor now.' She bit her lip, as though worried she might have offended her transhuman lord by wasting his time with something as trivial as mortal hierarchies, then added, tentatively: 'You remember me?'

'I seldom forget,' said Koorland. 'Thank the Emperor for designing me thus.'

'I... I will.'

'Praise be,' Bohemond murmured.

'Can I help you, proctor?'

'Yes, lord.' She snapped another salute and held it. 'The provost-colonel demands the return of Daylight Pad Theta to the Adeptus Arbites.'

'Tell her no.'

Haas smiled. 'Thank you, lord.'

With a growl, Bohemond turned his back on the woman who reached barely as high as his elbow and made to head back to his shuttle.

'They demand your protection, but only so long as you do not inconvenience *their* little fiefdoms. I leave you to it, brother, and may I never find myself embroiled in politics again.'

Koorland nodded his agreement. 'From my shuttle, I saw rioters outside of the Great Chamber itself. I am not surprised.'

'They should be put down,' rumbled the fourth Space Marine present, Eternity, standing at the near edge of the platform opposite Daylight. 'The expression of such dissent within the Palace grounds is a capital sin.'

The Black Templar who had become Eternity had demanded that wall and that duty, had insisted that he be the last line between the Custodes and the rest of the universe. He, more than anyone, served as a reminder that an Imperial Fist was more than just the colours that he wore. Haas looked towards the towering wall-brother, a sudden wariness, fear even, causing her face to tense, as if she had heard this particular Black Templar's voice before.

'Go to them then, brother,' said Koorland, turning to meet the glowing red lenses of Eternity's helm. 'Let them see that they are safe, that it is an Imperial Fist that walks amongst them.' He glanced to Haas. The woman was almost shaking, worse than when she had been rescued from the orks' captivity. 'Let them all see.'

THREE

Terra – the Imperial Palace

The Great Chamber had been the institutional heart of Terra for as long as Terra had been the heart of an Imperium of Man. At capacity, it could hold half a million citizens. It was a coliseum, a public arena of awesome scale, built to the grand demands of Unitarian dreams. The restoration work enacted in the aftermath of the Great Heresy had been largely sympathetic, cosmetic re-imaginings of the occasional mural where a pict of the original could not be found or showed an inconvenient contradiction to the Creed notwithstanding.

Vast tiers of empty seating surrounded a central dais. Twelve large chairs were spaced evenly across its centre line, backed by the heraldic banners of the twelve great pillars of Imperial government. A speaker's podium, raised by the spread wings of a golden aquila, glittered under the triangulated beams of focused lighting. The dais rotated almost imperceptibly, and a more potent metaphor for the pace of decision-making by said great pillars of Imperial government Vangorich could not imagine.

The last vestige of representative and accountable governance stood at the far east end of the chamber: a statue of the great Rogal Dorn, raised in commemoration by his brother, the first Lord Guilliman. The primarch watched the council of the day with an expression of infamous severity.

Drakan Vangorich was not a man given to idle dreams, but the thought of what a living, breathing primarch would make of the small men trying to fill their superhuman boots gave him a little pleasure.

'Order, please,' said Tobris Ekharth, Master of the Administratum, reading tiredly from the data-slate in his hands. His voice mumbled back to him on a time-delayed echo from the vox-casters set up around the vast auditorium. Small-arms fire in the distance – but not all *that* distant – broke up the carefully calibrated augmitter system with pernicious static. 'I'm sure that the situation is under control... I...'

He blinked myopically at a second data-slate on the lectern in front of him, then bent to listen to some aide unseen behind the beam-bright podium lights and visibly pulled himself together.

'I've been made aware that the situation is well in hand. If you could all now please access your agenda packets, cryptex key kappa-tribus-septum-septum-omega, and once we're all here we can begin.'

Scattered around the swathes of empty seating, lesser lords and meme-serfs approved by the Administratum's increasingly stringent vetting lists peeled the security tape off their packets and tapped in the cryptex key.

Vangorich did as everyone else did. As a man of medium

height and medium build, dressed in black with oiled-back black hair like any aide or staffer present, he was adept at discouraging notice. His skin shared the pale tone of the trillions who lived their lives on lightless Terra, his few features of note being his dark, wide-set eyes and a tiny scar that bridged the lower part of his face between jaw and chin.

He had, of course, memorised the contents of an unredacted version of the package, and his agents had furnished him with the cryptex key to the final document as soon as it had been disseminated amongst the High Twelve.

It had been a hundred years since a Grand Master of the Officio Assassinorum had been seated amongst that number, but one grew accustomed to certain privileges of access, particularly if one possessed the means to retain them. Indeed, Vangorich considered it the patriotic duty of his office to keep his finger, as the saying went, on the Senatorum's pulse.

Scanning the ninety-seven-page abstract, he flagged up the most glaring omissions from the original agenda. It was always an amusing mental exercise to attempt to deduce who was responsible for removing what.

A complaint from the Admiralty on the costs imposed on them by the transfer of the blockade from the Last Wall to the Navy? Fabricator General Kubik. Too easy. The Fabricator General would accept any cost to get his mechadendrites on the orks' technologies, particularly if it could be loaded onto another.

A demand for civilian evacuation of the cathedral world Madrilline? Lansung. Why discuss what you no longer had the ships in range to deliver?

A motion to restrict Chapter Master Koorland's 'disruptive' access to Naval facilities, and, reading between the lines, the Lucifer Blacks? It had the patrician fingers of the Paternoval Envoy all over it. Smiling archly, he skimmed ahead. The only downside was that Helad Gibran no longer owed him a favour. He held the page and frowned in thought. Here was an interesting omission.

A report of mass starvations in Albia Hive. Basic provisioning was the duty of the Administratum, but he didn't think that Ekharth had the spine for this kind of backroom politicking. Juskina Tull of the Chartist Captains, perhaps.

He glanced up to the dais.

Juskina Tull looked waxen under the podium lights, haunted by an enfolding horror that was so much worse from the other side of her glassy stare. Host to a magnificent gown of tented lace and emeralds, she had barely moved in half an hour. Just a telling blink of the eyes whenever the screams became loud enough, near enough, to escape the weapons fire. She wasn't hearing screams. She was hearing cries for blood.

No.

Definitely not Tull.

The other lords were still working their way to their seats.

Gibran, Paternoval Envoy of the Navigators, and Sark, the otherworldly Master of the Astronomican, were ushered into their allotted seats by plush-liveried Senatorum staff. Spread in his chair at the opposite end of the dais, Anwar of the Adeptus Astra Telepathica watched his fellow abhumans with a deep, probing gaze. The uncanny walked down Vangorich's spine with fingers of ice. Seated beside the Imperium's most powerful sanctioned psyker in full Astra Militarum dress uniform, the Lord Militant, Abel Verreault, attempted to make small talk.

A choir of cherubs and servo-seraphim hovered around the carved Albian oak podium doors. Beneath the dragonfly chirr of hymnals, Ecclesiarch Mesring and Lord Admiral Lansung entered together. Lansung had lately taken to porting his great bulk around with the aid of a silver cane, but his physical deterioration was barely noticeable beside that of the Ecclesiarch. Mesring looked feral. His hair was wild. His surplice was unpressed and clearly the same that he had worn to the previous week's session. There were purpling wine stains in his beard. The two men were arguing heatedly about fleet deployments to the Tang Sector, something that continued well after Senatorum aides had adroitly manoeuvred them to non-adjacent seats.

Provost-Colonel Chabil Sarrihya rolled her eyes as if despairing of the behaviour of children, checked her wrist-chrono augmetic, and continued pacing. Her superior in the Adeptus Arbites, Vernor Zeck, had unilaterally absented himself from Senatorum business once civil disobedience had spilled into the Sanctum Imperialis, and had preferred not to return since. His deputy had no resort to such sanction and knew it. So she paced back – clipped turn – and forth in front of Fabricator General Kubik. The representative of Mars was almost as still as his counterpart from the Merchant Fleets, mecha-dendrites tapping on his chair's arm interface in binarised counterpoint to the Provost-Colonel's steps.

Ekharth's timid appeal for order earned him a sharp look from Udin Macht Udo.

The Lord Commander of the Imperium, commander-in-chief of its incalculable assets of war and peace, simmered lamely in his grand throne. The slow pinkening of his face was accentuated by his shaved head, and the way the darkening turned the old scar that crossed the left side of his face and neck and through his milky eye an almost luminescent white. Though separate from and above any single military arm of the Imperium, he wore the starched white grand admiral's uniform of his previous career in the Navy. It practically burst with medals and overcompensation.

It was pathetic.

Only the Inquisitorial Representative was still absent.

'I suppose we could always just execute them all,' suggested the woman seated at Vangorich's right.

'A little extreme, perhaps.' A passing thought temporarily brightened his mind. 'But tempting.'

Commandant Ursula Cage of the Schola Progenium was a striking woman. As the joint senior commissar, she was a feared individual. The utilitarian lines of one of Terra's ancient noble houses shaped her face. Her hair was the shade and texture of gunmetal. She sat forwards, barely on her seat at all: summary justice *in potentia*.

'Name me one who doesn't deserve it.'

'Verreault means well.'

With a short, hard laugh, Cage reached inside her greatcoat's breast pocket and handed him a data-slate. It was a high-level briefing document with an Astra Militarum 'CONFIDENTIAL' stamp emblazoned across each page. The kind that were intercepted, copied, and subtly rerouted to Vangorich's desk about ten thousand times each day. He seldom read them personally. He made an exception for this one.

It was the usual bad news – worlds lost or, suddenly unresponsive, presumed so – but there were bright spots if one looked hard enough.

Some dogged defending of an ice world called Valhalla had checked one front of the orks' push into the Ultima Segmentum, and a small force of Ultramarines had successfully disabled an attack moon in orbit of Calth. Added to the one brought down by Admiral Lansung at Port Sanctus, and another by a combined force of Blood Angels and Novamarines, that made three confirmed kills.

Three. In a galaxy-wide incursion. No wonder they were losing. He didn't need another classified internal document to tell him that.

'The orks are getting sophisticated,' murmured Cage. 'Their choice of targets suggests a network of supply lines, resource processing centres and communication hubs that we've not seen before.' She smiled coldly. 'Or so the Progenium Tacticae tell us.'

'This wasn't in the unredacted agenda packet.'

She cocked an eyebrow. 'Everyone knows orks can *appear* intelligent in battle. I know. But in war?' She shook her head. 'The Lord Militant would have been laughed out of the Senatorum.'

Vangorich glanced over his shoulder as a squad of Lucifer Blacks in enamelled black carapace powered up their shock glaives and ran for the main doors. They were wearing yellow armbands. Vangorich had never seen anything like that in the regiment before. He filed a mental note to look into it.

'Why are you showing this to me?' he asked.

The Lucifer Blacks thumped through the transport-sized oak doors. Suddenly, the sound of bolter fire was very close indeed.

'Operational freedom,' said Cage. 'I have a certain amount of leeway. There are Progenium schools in the orks' path, Tempestus regiments that the Lord Militant doesn't know about, but you? I'm willing to bet you have agents in the area so deep even they don't know who they are.'

'This reputation of mine will get me into trouble one day.'

'I was told you had a sense of humour, Grand Master. One of many things I disapprove of.'

'And who told you such a thing?'

'Wienand.'

'You've spoken to Wienand?'

She ignored his question. 'We can't beat the orks without them.' She nodded towards the lords on the dais. 'But with organisations like ours we can slow them down.'

'Leave it with me,' Vangorich murmured, noncommittal, passing the slate back to the aide sitting in the pew immediately behind him.

Then, along with several hundred others in a hall built for half a million, he turned towards the sudden acrimony spilling from the dais.

Udo was rising, pulling the creases from his uniform in a clink of brass, and then glaring milkily from his throne.

The Inquisitorial Representative had arrived. Both of them.

Lastan Neemagiun Veritus walked up to the dais with a clunking, power-armoured stride. His antique battleplate was white, filigreed with theurgic symbols and possessed of its own wanton animus by fluttering papyrus scraps. The man himself was shrunken and pallid. His armour's gorget seals sucked and wheezed about his thoat like a ventilator. At his shoulder, walking briskly and without augmentation, came a woman with short, pale grey hair and a face far younger than her eyes.

Vangorich had never considered her appearance to be anything other than ordinary until just then, and the kick of his emotional rebuke surprised him.

'*Wienand,*' he breathed.

Udin Macht Udo puffed out his medals. 'The names of all Senatorum aides are to be pre-submitted to the Administratum for approval.' Lips curled back, he turned his dead eye onto Ekharth, who quickly blathered his agreement. 'Inquisitor Wienand will have to leave.'

'She is not my aide,' said Veritus, his voice like sand. 'She is the Inquisitorial Representative.'

'Not any more, Veritus. You are.'

'Until the Inquisition decides otherwise,' said Wienand smoothly.

Veritus had an undeniable gravitas, an automatic authority brought on by age and ceramite, but Wienand spoke with a reasoned clarity that the Senatorum had been missing for too long. 'And now it has been decided that Lastan and I *both* will best represent our organisation at this time.'

'Outrageous!' spat Mesring, jumping from his chair like a feral cat. 'This is a grab for power.'

'Agreed,' came Kubik's unsubtle vocalisation.

Wienand spread her hands peaceably. 'The Inquisition still has one vote on this council.'

'But two voices,' whispered Anwar, silkily.

'United,' said Veritus. 'As it is time we all were.'

The Provost-Colonel was speaking urgently into a vox-pin in her cuff. Lansung appeared to be nodding slowly in agreement.

A hush had fallen over the auditorium, all eyes on Udin Macht Udo as the Lord Guilliman turned and strode stiff-backed from the podium.

'Well, sir,' said Beast Krule, pushing his thick arms over Vangorich's seat back and secreting the commissar's data-slate into one of several concealed pockets. 'I'd say that makes things interesting.'

FOUR

Mars – Pavonis Mons

Two masked, metal-skinned skitarii marched Eldon Urqui-dex's awkward frame down the long, smearily-lit corridor. The clump of their stride rattled the loose, metallic floor and swished the hems of their robes. The tough, energy-damping weave of their garments did odd things to the incident light, darkening their deep crimson hue to just a shade above black. These were alphas, veterans drawn from the numberless battle maniples of Mars and augmented according to that status. The best.

The transorganic soldiers' long march brought them to a door, airlock-solid, guarded by another fearsomely augmeti-cised warrior-build in dark robes and wielding a brass-plated heavy rifle that bristled with deadly technologies. An arc rifle. Perfect for the close-range, narrow-quarters combat that a probability engine might envisage for the labyrinthine laboratorium subplex of Pavonis Mons. The best.

The dim red glow of the guard's visored sight washed over Urquidex. Sour air, five parts per million perspiration, five hundred parts engine grease, rasped in and out of his cognis filters. The guard brought around his rifle in a nightingale murmur of high-tech servos and synthetics. At that range, with that weapon, with those cortico-sensory enhancements, aim was unnecessary.

They weren't going to kill him.

Easier to have done it in any one of a hundred different places before now. The three-hour cage descent into the post-industrial hive of Pavonis crater. The skim pad, dust-blown and radiation-scoured, nothing beneath it for miles but stratified piping and still-radioactive sludge. Aboard the dust skimmer, laser-etched with the signum of the 1014 Noctis Maniple, that had swept him over the ancient rust sands and light harvesters of the Martian desert. Or even right there in his plug station in the Noctis Labyrinth where they had come for him. Who would have tried to stop them, or cared if he had been summarily executed even as he ordered his files? The locum trajectorae? His fellow adepts?

As well to expect an impassioned defence from the tech-servitors.

They weren't going to kill him.

The Assassin, Yendl, must have been unmasked and now Van Auken wanted to interrogate her accomplice in person: that was the only explanation that made sense. Urquidex forced his dry mouth to swallow. His thoughts were of nerve endings and pain receptors: trillions of microscopic sensors, thousands of kilometres of insulated wiring, all evolutionarily perfected by the goal of rendering the hominids of his direct antecedence sufficiently risk-averse to perpetuate Eldon Urquidex. But now, no further.

The guard bared his metal palm to the judgement of the reader by the door. There was a clunk, a ripple through the creaking substructure, then a gasp of air as the doors cracked ajar and then shunted apart. His escorts led him through. They were not unkind.

Force was mass, velocity, and an exponent.

Kindness did not factor.

The chamber on the other side of the door was a short octagonal cylinder, like an expressionistic version of an antique eight-shot's firing cylinder portrayed through geometry. The ceiling and main walls were a ridged metal, some kind of supplementary ventilation system running along the recesses. The floor was the same loose, rattling metal slats as it had been outside. The angled slants joining the horizontals to the verticals were of a browning armourglass.

'Stop here,' grated the skitarius to his right.

He stopped there.

The two skitarii backed away through the door. The guard simultaneously lowered his own weapon and punched the control panel to bring the doors to a shuddering close. Urquidex stared at the solid plasteel for a moment, feeling an utterly illogical sense of panic on watching the two skitarii leave, as if they had been not colluders in his captivity, but protectors, the only thing standing between him and death.

He shivered, the tensile fibres bonding his digitools directly into his nervous system causing them to twitch accordingly. Unsure what else to do, he swallowed and shuffled around to face the opposite door.

There was a clank, as if he had triggered something with

his movement, and an intense ultraviolet light flooded in through the armourglass. He grunted in pain. His instinct was to turn away and he did so, optics down, but the light was coming from everywhere. It was purple, piercing, retina-burning, but at the same time little more than bleedthrough, an augur ghost at the edge of his perceptual range. The effect was at once vivid and watery. Biologis adepts designated the treatment as 'soft' decontamination: degrade any biological contaminant, while leaving precious technologies intact and without chemical residual.

Urquidex retracted his telescopic eyestalks and dialled their sensitive optics shut, burying his face in the folds of his robes for good measure. He could feel his exposed flesh begin to heat. This biological contaminant did not consider the procedure nearly as soft as it once had.

At the same time, he became aware of an urgent hiss. Some kind of gas was being delivered into the chamber through that secondary ventilation system. His heart rate spiked, a fight or flight reflex that perversely then delivered the command for his lungs to draw deep. Ozone, he realised, sensing the epithelial sting on the lining of his nose. Urquidex felt his UV-reddened skin begin to burn.

The lights shut down abruptly. The hiss stopped.

Cautiously, Urquidex re-extended his eyes. He could still smell ozone, a sore-throat tightness down the back of his mouth.

'Proceed, magos.'

The voice was female, piped into the chamber like gas through the walls.

A clunk sounded from the far end of the cubicle, followed

by a whoosh of evacuating air. Urquidex winced as it flowed over his sunburned flesh and the door ground open. His ears popped under the change in pressure.

A biologis laboratorium, then: the design adhered to schemata laid down by arch-magi from an era before the Dark Age of Technology, and to Urquidex was more familiar than his own surgically modified face. A slender needle of curiosity pricked his skin of fear. Such a place was an unlikely venue for an interrogation, or even an execution.

He walked through the door to be met by another skitarius. This one was female, that much of her original body plan evident even through her heavy robes and obtrusive techno-refinements, and was covering the door with an arc pistol. Her left hand had been retrofitted with a combat glove with an integrated transonic razor. Urquidex absorbed those prosaic details at a glance, for her most unique feature was too stunning to devote time and attention elsewhere. Head to toe, the skitarius had been physically remodelled in dazzling silver. Other agencies of the Imperium exploited that precious metal for its anti-psychic properties, but the Adeptus Biologis archives retained many fragmentary references to its ancient bactericidal application.

She watched him sceptically, and Urquidex, fearfully, said nothing.

'Stand down to readiness level, Zeta-One Prime,' came the deep, breathy voice of Artisan Trajectorae Van Auken, each word enunciated with a puff of mechanical diaphragms.

Eldon stiffened and froze.

The artisan trajectorae emerged from the incense pall that cloaked a bank of shuddering ruminators. His spindly shoulders were slumped under the weight of a servo-harness and multitools, and his forehead had been broadened and deepened with the installation of a thick plasteel plate. He emitted a hiss of pistoned air and dismissed his sterile and glittering adjutant with the flex of a mechadendrite.

'You have no questions, magos? Do you forget the Eleventh Universal Law?'

Urquidex answered by rote. 'The universe is uncertain until it is observed.'

'Your locum trajectorae expressed concerns regarding your state of mind. It was her conclusion that you were distracted, that the Grand Experiment was in some way insufficiently fulfilling.'

Urquidex opened his mouth, but there was no subjective rebuttal to the locum trajectorae's objective conclusions. He remained silent, mouth dry. *Van Auken knew.* The thought ran round and round his higher functions like a scrapcode algorithm on a recursive loop.

'You are frustrated by the lack of progress,' Van Auken continued for him. 'I understand. It is not your proper specialism. You have been unable to devote your full energies to this grand task.'

'Yes, artisan,' he said carefully. 'But my lapse of purpose is inexcusable.'

'Indeed so, but the Fabricator General has another task more meritous of your talents, magos.'

The artisan trajectorae turned and for the first time, Urquidex took a proper look at the glorious scale of the laboratorium.

Instruments filled the floor, spaced apart from one

another, as machines of their type were known to be jealous of their status within the schemata, and could be cantankerous when the proper attention was not afforded them. Adepts of the first level chanted soothing psalms, scattering the straining machines with crystals from their aspersoria, carbon dioxide produced and sanctified in the manufactories of Marcotis Temple. Even so, electrical smoke seeped from the instruments' backs and pooled on the metal tiles. Wheezing scrubbers did their best to filter the pollutants from the air.

Servitors clumped from instrument to instrument carrying plastek plates indented with tiny wells containing organic serum. Attendant techno-magi received the sample dishes, commended them to the all-seeing attentions of the Omnissiah, and fed them into the machines under their care. And through the semi-transparent plastek view-plates that overlooked the sterilisation chamber, the exact repetitive routine was enacted over and over, identically laid out levels stacked one atop the next high into the smog layer.

'Samples are brought to this laboratorium from across the Imperium,' said Van Auken. 'You can understand the demand for secrecy. And for biological integrity.'

Urquidex nodded.

A magos was loading a set of plates into the ornately inscribed chrome housing of a prognosticator, triggering seizures of clacking and shuddering and frenzied bursts of laser light. In parallel, hundreds of sequence graphics sputtered up on the networked displays. Each was an assemblage of coloured lines representing As and Ts, Cs and Gs, and Xs. After about half an hour of chewing noises the machine expelled the spent samples and emitted an insatiable peal for more data.

'You hope to find a solution to the Grand Experiment in their genetic code,' said Urquidex. 'It won't work. *Veridi giganticus*' genome is structurally unstable. It is a mosaic of recombinatorial sequences and mobilisable elements, continually on the cusp of one speciation event or another. *Veridi giganticus* should not be at all.'

'It is your specialism, magos, not mine, and I do not pretend to understand it. But no, that is not our goal.'

With his human hand Van Auken directed Urquidex's attention to a neighbouring screen. This one was packed with moving code lines, the backing cogitator plugged via a heavy-duty shunt into a run of cabling that disappeared into the ceiling. The system's program wafer had the machine data-mining the Martian noosphere, pulling up astropathic logs, engagement reports, every bit of data relevant to the *Veridi giganticus* samples that came with a grid stamp and a time stamp, and then cross-referencing them against the sequence output.

A map.

The artisan trajectorae was making a map.

The very genetic instability of *Veridi giganticus* was the way in. A population would be expected to accumulate sequence alterations over a very short period of time. As they moved on and established new populations, those unique alterations would be carried forward and added to, and so on. With enough samples those changes could be tracked back. The Adeptus Biologis did it all the time. Mapping the spread of viruses through hive worlds, extrapolating the evolution of newly discovered *Homo* sub-species at the request of the Inquisition. Thus was the grace of the Omnissiah made manifest in the base material of Its organic machines.

Urquidex could see sample tags referenced to Arda-mantua, Undine, Malleus Mundi. Hundreds, thousands of names: worlds from the breadth and span of the Impe-rium. The ork incursion was more widespread even than he had realised.

'You are looking for the orks' home world.'

'One successful test does not complete the Grand Exper-iment. Phobos has a diameter of twenty-two kilometres. Mars is more than three hundred and ten times larger. In effect, the Grand Experiment has become an issue of scale.'

'Scale...'

Urquidex tested the word, measured it, weighed it. The Grand Experiment had not stalled because of him or Yendl. It was a technical problem. Yendl was probably still alive, going over his last communiqué and wondering what had become of him. He swallowed, his sudden relief somehow more powerful even than his fear had been, and clasped his hands behind his back to obscure his quivering digitools.

'*Veridi giganticus* has somehow managed to overcome the discontinuity between efficiency and scale,' said Van Auken. 'Or otherwise devised a solution to circumvent the Omnissiah's constants.'

'It sounds as though you admire them for it.'

'They are a superbly constructed species, individually adaptive, collectively diverse. They are an apex species, magos, as once we were. There is much to re-learn from them, and yes, we are not above admiration. We have narrowed their point of origin to six or seven candidate sectors. A few thousand systems at the galactic core of Ultima Segmentum.'

Urquidex's mind spun out a stream of hurried calculations. Stars came fast and close in the core and a few thousand systems need not, comparatively at least, cover a lot of space. A search of it would still be a massive logistical undertaking, but compared to the galaxy as a whole...

'Has the Imperium been informed?'

'The Fabricator General will apprise them if and when the timing is opportune. The Imperium is more than Terra, magos, and humanity is more than the Imperium. We must learn how *Veridi giganticus* operate their technology. You were there on Ardamantua. The Eleventh Universal Law applies. You have observed *Veridi giganticus*. They are not unknown to you.'

Eldon nodded mutely, numbly. The instruments before him continued to gorge on the galaxy of data they were being fed. Too much to smuggle to Terra. Far too much. He had to find the world.

One world. One word.

That, he could get to Yendl. And to Terra.

FIVE

Uandis System – Mandeville point

Targeting solutions crowded the lower right quadrant of *Dantalion*'s main viewer, coloured box reticules jostling over the vid-feed of the cannibalised Oberon-class battleship. Energy sources. Weapons arrays. Structural weaknesses. Void-suited strategium serfs worked furiously to keep the display updated as the two vessels sailed into weapons range. Lobbed shells blistered *Dantalion*'s forward shields. Fire broke out between them as the two warships closed and slowly, slowly, began to turn apart. The Oberon-class dropped to port, *Dantalion* climbed to starboard, both ships manoeuvering to present the massed firepower of their broadsides. Banks of hardlines provided wired communications between *Dantalion*'s command deck and the thousands of weapons hardpoints, loading bays, and cogitators throughout the two-kilometre-long battle-barge. Breathless operators called in status reports.

'Prow beamers charged and locked.'

'Macro-cannons trained to target.'

'Launch tubes alpha through delta report cyclonic war-heads loaded and ready at your mark.'

'Hold torpedos,' Shipmaster Marcarian commanded. 'Macro-weaponry and beamers only until we have the measure of their shields. Steady as she goes.'

'Fire weapons!' Zerberyn snarled.

'Firing, aye.'

White-hot beams of stellar fury drilled from *Dantalion*'s fusion batteries at near-light speed. The gap between the two ships had narrowed to a few thousand kilometres – an almost terrestrial scale, a space of particle fire and scrambled fighter craft – and the barrage hit almost instanta-neously. The first beam strike overloaded the Oberon-class' jury-rigged void shield array. The second lanced through the outer hull, and set off chain explosions within the super-structure. The fusion beamers fired in sequence. Each blast lasted split seconds before the collider cells had to be removed to be cooled and recharged, but the relative velocities and opposing vectors meant that those snap shots were sufficient to gouge through hundreds of metres of armour cladding.

Spewing drive plasma and the atomised constituents of its outer hull, the Oberon-class sailed under *Dantalion*'s belly, the battle-barge yawing over its blistered prow.

'Ventral batteries report locks.'

'Fire!'

Sustained firepower chewed up the cannibalised vessel's dorsal plating. Atmospheric decompression ignited like the pilot light of a super-heavy flamer. Edged with greens, yel-lows and purples from vaporised hull elements, fire erupted into the void. For all *Dantalion*'s killing might, however, the honour of the ship-kill and the steel plaque on the wall of her shipmaster's cell fell to another.

'Shipmaster Akienas, of the *Paragon*, hailing,' Marcarian exclaimed, panting with short bursts of relieved laughter. 'It's the fleet.'

The cheers of those on the command deck followed the aegis frigate *Paragon* as she cut across her parent ship's nose. Engine stacks on full burn whited out *Dantalion*'s viewer and for a moment the escort passed close enough that the electromagnetic distortion generated by the interplay of the two sets of shields whined over every open channel.

Zerberyn did not cheer. He had never doubted, and there was little to celebrate in seeing others catch up to one's certainty.

The escort sailed under as *Dantalion* went over. The dying Oberon-class battleship cruised between them, trailing plasma discharge and colour distortions as *Paragon* opened up. Anti-fighter batteries walked down her centre line at devastatingly close range. They struck something critical, an unsecured mega-weapon or a main plasma chamber of the drive core.

The battleship detonated like an atomic warhead.

Dantalion blazed inside her shields like a model voidship in a lightning cage. *Paragon*'s layered shielding failed simultaneously in an explosive moment of brilliance that rivalled the birth of a star. Her starboard side buckled under forced compression. Bent plates spewed atmosphere, and she skewed off wildly on a new trajectory.

Unshielded ork fighter-bombers that had been emptied out of the Oberon-class' flight decks were simply obliterated. Muzzle-flash explosions dotted the cloud of attack craft that had been racing in behind. The survivors broke off their run under the barrage of *Dantalion*'s flak guns and scattered, weaving a craze of propellant tails behind them.

'Track them, shipmaster, see where they go,' said Zerberyn. 'Move to cover *Paragon* and raise Akienas.'

'Helm, new heading,' Marcarian relayed. 'Put us between *Paragon* and the orks, siphon power to starbord shields, mobilise reserve gunnery teams to dorsal, starboard and ventral flak batteries.'

The command deck, already a hive of purpose, set about the new orders with a well-drilled efficiency.

'Aye sir, new heading. Plotting turn.'

'No response from *Paragon*.'

'Reading catastrophic damage to her primary transceiver array. Trying to contact her machine-spirit.'

On the main viewer, the wreckage of the Oberon-class slowly dispersed.

'The beacon?' said Zerberyn, impatiently.

'Nothing yet, lord.'

'Lords!' The elated cry came from the vox-liaison. She tore off her headphones, and leapt out of her chair. 'Fists Exemplar ships incoming. *Chastened. Angel Astra. Unbroken.* It's the whole fleet.'

'Bright skies,' Marcarian murmured, and closed his good eye.

'Show me,' said Zerberyn.

The vid-feed in the oculus switched to a view dorsal aft. There were bits of coiled wire, ice-encrusted cosmic dust that had accumulated around the communication vanes, and macro-turrets around the edge of the image. Beyond the fuzz, a dozen iron-grey splinters hung in space, ranging from aegis frigates a few hundred metres long to mighty strike cruisers a kilometre in length and bristling with armament enough to waste a planetary hemisphere. Explosive shells and high-energy plasma spat between them and the loose agglomeration of ork cruisers that had strayed this far from the main battle area.

The most likely theoretical was they were a picketing force set to guard the Mandeville point. To what end, Zerberyn could only speculate, but if he was indulging in theoreticals then he might further suppose that it was to ensure that whomever it was currently engaged by the main ork battlegroup did not escape the system.

More warships translated in all the time, cutting through the empyreal sheath like knives through black silk. Each new arrival brought a burst of vox-chatter that gabbled from the vox-turret hardlines and bled into the general commotion. Void-suited tacticians hurried to update the strategium desk, while vox-personnel spoke on two, or sometimes three, lines at once in an effort to impose the pre-formulated formation protocols on the emerging fleet.

It had been for just a few short decades that the Fists Exemplar had called Eidolica their home, but for seven centuries prior their home range had been the Rubicante Flux. Their fleet was sizeable. With the exclusion of the Black Templars, whose numbers were a secret guarded even amongst brothers, the Fists Exemplar provided over half of the Last Wall's naval power.

Zerberyn was not of a mind to let them forget it.

A huge shape slid into main view, high on *Dantalion*'s z-axis.

Serfs from every station rose in unison to clap and cheer it. It was a battle-barge, *Dantalion*'s sister ship, but even more heavily armed. Kilometre after battle-scarred kilometre of adamantium-grey crenellations bristled with macro-batteries like the armour studs on a chrono-gladiator. Gothic spires rose from its central bulk, counterbalanced by smaller ventral towers. Launch tubes, flak turrets and antennae arrays vied with the asteroid-pitted statues of warrior angels aboard the immense dorsal spine. A volley of torpedo launches from her broadside tore a slow-turning ork crusier to shreds. *Dantalion* rocked with the energy discharge.

'*Alcazar Remembered*,' Marcarian confirmed with one half of a smile.

'Welcome the Chapter Master,' said Zerberyn in a voice that offered little of the kind. 'Transmit our tactical data to the flagship.'

The vox-liaison frowned as she retook her seat, refitted her headset, and swivelled back to her console. Zerberyn joined her at her station.

'A priority transmission,' she reported. 'It's coming through some intense interference, but it's definitely Last Wall.'

'Our beacon?'

She shook her head as she worked. 'The coordinates don't tally. The beacon was being transmitted from a near-stationary position much closer to the Vandis star.

This signal is new, and it's coming from the system's edge.' She stood and shouted at the liaison working auspectoria, then dropped back into her seat as the requested read-outs squirted across to her system. 'Residual warp backwash from twenty to twenty-five vessels suggests a recent inbound translation. An hour old, maximum. Multiple radiation sources, plasma discharge, particle spread suggestive of hostile tractor locks on ships running full ahead.' She spun her chair towards Zerberyn and leant back to look up to him. 'It's a Black Templars fleet, my lord, inbound on the beacon at ninety degrees to our position. Auto-identifiers name the signalling ship the *Interdictor*.'

'Can I speak to them?'

'I can't guarantee you'll hear every word.'

'Put it on.'

The woman flicked a switch, and angry static roared from the turret's augmitters. The sounds of alien voices blizzarded across the channel, bleedthrough from neighbouring frequencies, some breathless prattle that ran and ran and ran.

Gorkamorkagorkamorka.

'Castellan Kasemund,' scratched the interference-punished voice of a Space Marine. Zerberyn could pick up only odd words of what followed. 'Crusade... recall... Phall... retaliation beacon... cruiser, *Obsidian Sky*... venerable...'

The castellan stopped speaking as static erased his words like ripple patterns on a beach as the moons pulled the tide higher.

Gorkamorkagorkamorkagorkamorka.

'They must have been in the materium when they received *Obsidian Sky*'s transmission,' explained the vox-liaison. 'Most likely they would have received the complete message.'

Zerberyn nodded his understanding. 'Your strength and situation, brother?'

Gorkamorkagorkamorka.

'Eleven ships... Crusade... spear in the belly... boarded... push us hard... not show the xenos our backs.'

The spit and pop of bolter fire imposed itself over the background crackle, but neither that nor the orkish chatter could quite disguise the Black Templar's uncomplicated disdain for the alien.

'Lord captain, sir,' mumbled Marcarian. 'Auspectoria confirms several hundred large-mass warships, twice that in escorts and support craft. It's inconceivable that one ship could have survived.'

'And yet the battle rages on.'

Zerberyn thought back on the picket fleet the orks had positioned to hold the Mandeville point, and presumably the other that the Black Templars had broken through. The incredible mobilisation of materiel to run down one ship.

It was the work of a moment, a moment in which the command deck buzzed with a thousand and one operations.

'*Bulwark* and *Faceless Warrior* coming astern.'

'The orks are pulling back their fighters. They're breaking off.'

'Orders from the Chapter Master to hold this line while *Noble Savage* takes *Paragon* under tow.'

The image on the main view had switched again, this time to a starboard shot. *Dantalion*'s broadside lit up with detonations as her macrocannons opened fire in unison.

Zerberyn felt the battle-barge pushed several metres to port. Void flares and feedback flashed across the viewer as *Dantalion* traded fire with a pair of brutish ork battlecruisers, box-jawed with weapon blisters and extraneous plating. The astern battlecruiser came apart under a volley of prow lances and void torpedos as *Bulwark* slid into position.

There was some reason the orks wanted to keep the *Obsidian Sky* inside this system.

'I have them,' cried Vox. '*Obsidian Sky* and one other vessel. Her spirit resists divulging her identity, but energy profiles and mass ratios suggest an Adeptus Astartes cruiser.'

The turret augmitters fizzed with vox-corruption. 'Incoming... Throne... massive... protects–'

'Castellan? Castellan?'

Gorkamorkagorkamorkagorkamorkagorkamorka.

'Cut it off.'

The augmitters hissed like the animated dead, and then went silent.

'Should I apprise *Alcazar Remembered*, lord?' asked Marcarian.

'Of course, but first signal to *Bulwark* and *Faceless Warrior*.'

'To what end, lord?'

An appalled exclamation drew Zerberyn and his shipmaster's attention towards the chart desk before he could answer. Strategium serfs backed away from it as though afraid that it was one of them that had damaged it. A small portion of the display had been blacked out: a sphere of unidentifiable darkness moved slowly through the glowing hololith field towards the highlighted wedge of Black

Templars ships, ork icons disappearing as though swallowed by a black hole.

'The incoming vessel that the *Interdictor* reported,' Zerberyn concluded.

Marcarian looked to him, aghast. 'What kind of monster does it carry?'

'Contact *Bulwark* and *Faceless Warrior*. Advise them to break formation and follow us.'

'But lord, Thane's orders–'

'Are subordinate to an Exemplar's judgement. We must protect the *Obsidian Sky*.' Zerberyn glanced back to the chart desk, the auspex shadow that was slowly spreading across it. He could almost hear the challenge of the Beast roared across light years. 'We must engage that ship.'

'Try again,' commanded Maximus Thane, Chapter Master of the Fists Exemplar. 'I want my ships back in formation.'

'They're not responding, lord Chapter Master.'

'Is Zerberyn ignoring me?'

'It's the interference, lord. It's getting worse and *Dantalion*'s already out of contactable range. I'm not getting a reply from *Bulwark* or *Faceless Warrior* either.'

Maximus Thane leaned forward, one hissing, armoured boot up on the seat of his command throne as though being seated was a transient luxury that he might abjure at a moment's notice.

In the auspectoria turret below, void-suited serfs bent over the crowded scanner table, wielding protractors and slide rules with the prowess of champions at the Festival of Blades, calling out number strings to their colleagues mobbing the chart desk at the neighbouring strategium turret. The blisters of colour-coded ork markers at the desk's extreme range were beginning to drop off the hololithic display, and operators shouted across one another in their efforts to explain why.

To Thane it resembled a planetary transition; a slow-moving disc that temporily blanked out a small portion of its parent sun.

Compared to the mortal men and women under his authority he was an armoured giant, face stern, battleplate grey as weathered bedrock, enthroned within a cathedra of moulded steel and shock-responsive hydraulics. From the various read-outs and data-displays that sprouted from the armrests, he could monitor every major function of the ship from shield strength to engine efficiency to oxygen pressure. His oversight was total, his command absolute. He was brilliant, naturally, but tactical aptitude could be found at every level of the Chapter. There were plenty, also – Zerberyn or Dentor (*Daylight* now, he reminded himself) to name but two – with greater prowess at arms. But there were none more stubborn, even amongst the elite ranks of his peers, and his perfectionist streak was as sharp as the high polish of his combat knife.

'My line of battle, shipmaster. Send forward *Grey Ranger* to hold *Dantalion*'s position.'

'Orders already relayed, lord.'

Shipmaster Weylon Kale was an old hand. He had served in the Crantar VII compliance, duelled ships with Archon M'awrr, and was even rumoured to have been aboard the old *Alcazar Astra* as a young subaltern during the Eidolican

Crash that had cost the Chapter the great Oriax Dantalion. Clasping his hands behind his back, the shipmaster turned to regard the main viewer that dominated the far prow-end of the command deck.

The large multi-screen display currently showed the unaugmented glitter of space and occasional sweeps of static. Without magnification, even a void fight between capital-class warships could lose itself in the deep black between stars. Vandis was the simmering red backdrop to most of the displays. The sun's surface churned, boiled, vented off the last of its fading heat. It was near enough to the fight to force the orks' battleships into a looser than usual formation to avoid arcing ejections of coronal matter, an uncommon display of self-preservation that Thane took into tactical consideration. One corner of the display had been given over to a view of the dead Oberon-class cruiser. The frigates *Chastened* and *Noble Savage* drove through the debris field, shields stuttering, as they slowly drew the wreck of *Paragon* out under tow.

A keystroke from Thane reformatted the subscreen to a schematic view of the Fists Exemplar fleet.

Frigates were moving ahead of the main fleet assets to present a picket of anti-fighter and anti-torpedo capability, but had already become mired in close fighting with the orks' own screening ships. The cruiser *Grey Ranger* was moving up as ordered to provide close support. Scrolling updates reported shield hits, weapons fire. Of the light ships, only the specialist frigate *Excelsior* held back, escorted by a pair of attack-dog-like frigates of her own. His fingers brushed the data-display again. The view zoomed out to show three golden aquilae, led by *Dantalion*, veering off towards the second, smaller Black Templars force that was stuck in the mass of ork warships like a splinter in a grox's belly.

A low-yield, shield-diffused impact trembled through the hull.

'What is Zerberyn thinking?'

Kale turned, hangdog face tilting to find Thane's above the command throne. 'I would not care to theorise as to the First Captain's thoughts, my lord. But *Dantalion*'s last data-burst reported the coordinates of *Obsidian Sky* and something about an ork flagship of some kind incoming. From his current vector I'd suggest he's attempting to flank this ship or perhaps lure it away from the Black Templars.'

'He's forced my hand.' Thane shifted in his throne so that both boots were grounded and he was leaning forward. He steepled his gauntleted fingers and growled. 'So we might as well act before we lose three more ships for no gain at all. Deploy the fleet, shipmaster, attack formation. Objective, the *Obsidian Sky* and her mysterious escort.'

Without a word, Kale turned on his heels, pointed across the deck to the vox-liaison, and produced a 'go' order with a nod. The dozen or so crew-serfs staffing the tiered, organ-like switchboard sprang into activity, routing wires, establishing vox-contacts, all under the close scrutiny of a red-robed tech-adept and a young-looking subaltern named Teal.

'*Dutiful*, reporting ready.'

'*Gulliman*, reporting ready.'

'*Unbroken*, reporting ready.'

'*Grey Ranger*, sir,' said Teal, breaking the litany and looking up from the control board to relay the message herself. 'The signal's breaking up, but she's reporting heavy shelling from beyond the range of her auspex. Requesting permission to break formation.'

'The orks cannot be actively targeting her at that kind of range,' said Thane. 'Permission denied.'

'Fishing,' murmured Kale. 'Hoping for a bite.'

'And they shall receive one. Instruct all ships, forward on us.' Thane clenched both gauntlets on his throne's armoured rests and rose. 'Ahead full, shipmaster, weapons free.'

Alcazar Remembered was a dominant beast. Her deck plates trembled with the power output required to sustain her formidable array of weapons systems and shields. She did not purr; she growled. It was difficult to stand aboard her as her engine stacks were fired to capacity and not share something of that invulnerability.

Her killing spirit vibrated through Thane's boots, into the core of his being like the might and will of the primarch himself.

'Sir.' The call came from the liaison working at auspectoria. 'We have visual on *Obsidian Sky*.'

'On screen.'

The images currently cycling through the main viewer cut out. The panoramic shot that replaced them was badly pixellated, as though translated from an image intended for a much smaller display. Blizzards of static swept across the screens at intervals. But there was no mistaking what they were seeing. A hush descended. Hazard and proximity alerts continued to bleep. Consoles chirruped for attention. Crew serfs pulled headsets from their ears and stared up at the screen in horror. Thane realised his hand had moved across his mouth.

It was the *Obsidian Sky*. They were watching her final moments.

In the cold silence of full magnification, a sequence of explosions blossomed from her port stern. Shields were gone. Bits of enamelled black outer hull glittered around her, held to her mass like a miniature ring system around a gas giant. The image shook slightly and fuzzed, as if the force of the blasts had somehow carried over the feed. The static bomb faded slowly. Tracers spat back and forth over the display. Sitting above *Obsidian Sky* and, relative to *Alcazar Remembered*, behind it, was another Adeptus Astartes cruiser. Their hulls were as close together as though conducting a last stand: two old warriors, back-to-back and beset by foes. A torpedo hit blasted a chunk from its dorsal spire. A tortured flare of combusting atmosphere raged into the airless void, spraying *Obsidian Sky* with metal fragments.

Thane leaned to the edge of his throne, elbows to the thigh plates of his armour, chin to his ceramite-clad knuckles.

Impossible.

'Traitors of the Fourth.'

The inconceivability of it brought a shiver to Thane's heart. He felt short of breath, his chest felt tight. The bald fact of what he was witnessing, that which was verifiable, that which was practical, simply could not overcome his disbelief in it.

Thane tightened his hold on the brass grip-studs. Focus on the immediate.

His voice, when it came, was the exemplar of strength. 'Signal *Obsidian Sky*.'

'I can't, my lord,' cried Teal, little trace of that invulnerability in her tone now. 'The interference is too intense.'

'Forward grids.' Kale's voice, coming from somewhere, some universe where Black Templars and Iron Warriors did not fight side-by-side. 'Keep those fighters off our shoulder.'

'Reduce magnification,' said Thane. 'Can you show me *Interdictor* and the main Black Templars fleet?'

'Aye, sir.'

The screen blinked to a broader view.

A dozen Black Templars vessels of various classes came into active view, the swollen chromosphere of Vandis highlighting lance arrays, fins and turrets in bitter red. They moved in an arrowhead formation, the blunted point pushing towards *Obsidian Sky* and the Iron Warriors cruiser, but were blocked off and encircled by ork ships. Debris clouds filled the gaping holes in their formation. Ork gunships, muscular and tusked, surrounded them, bristling with firepower. A Black Templars destroyer was in the final stages of disintegration, a bite taken out of its belly by the boarding claw of a monstrous ironclad. All inertial control lost, the two ships slowly spun around their conjoined axis as the void fight raged around them. The thump of explosions lit the screen, energy lances and the spent heat of solid rounds filling the display like embers rising off a fire.

And closing in on their position, casting a shadow light-minutes long, was a vessel that dwarfed them all.

'*Hellsteeth*.'

Thane was not sure who said it. It seemed to hiss out of

the internal communications, out of the unattended speakers and microphones of Vox. He had seen the ork attack moon that had demolished Eidolica, and the even larger war-engine that now loomed over Terra. They had been massive, but they had been moons. The gut accepted that they would be huge, even if the mind knew them to be constructed. They had been planetary bodies. He had processed them on that scale.

This was different. The behemoth hoving into view in pursuit of the Black Templars fleet was a *ship*. To be precise it was a carrier, fighters and destroyer-sized warships streaming from cavernous flight bays in its underside. It made the *Eternal Crusader* look like a corvette. Even the *Phalanx* would have been dwarfed.

Thane had no frame of reference for it.

A contemptuous slice from an axial beam weapon sheared through the aft of the rearmost Black Templars cruiser. Some kind of gravitic conversion beam, it crushed the entire aft section as though it were parchment scrap. The sudden spike of hypergravity flipped the warship nose to stern, torsional stresses cutting through what was left like a gladius through a ration can and spilling its contents into space.

Thane had never seen a weapon like it. Nothing the Imperium could produce came close. A sail-like array of adjusting fins, turning wheels, shivering wires and enormous copper rods rose from the ork carrier's bloated hull. A wash of strange, green-tinged energy sparked through the array towards its vertex and seemed to radiate into space. Thane's throat clenched.

Witch.

'All Black Templars identifiers are in,' said Auspectoria. He spoke quietly, mournfully, eyes on the on-screen tableau. 'Nine ships, and debris mass-equivalent to about fifteen more.'

Thane counted quickly.

'I see ten ships.'

'Nine ships, my lord. There's a delay. The feed is being relayed from *Excelsior*. Our systems can't penetrate the interference.'

The carrier fired again. A full spread of crude but devastingly effective torpedoes blasted another cruiser to pieces.

Nine.

'Can she relay a hololith signal? Can she get me *Obsidian Sky*?'

'I... I think so.'

'Then do it!'

Shipmaster Kale moved purposefully towards the strategium board. Another impact to the forward shields almost threw him the final metre, forcing him to steady himself against the metallic rim of the console's bulk housing. An armsman in grey carapace bodyplate and with a pump-action shotgun hanging from a shoulder strap hurried to help him. Kale thanked him with a curt nod, then gestured him back to his post.

'Should we also attempt to raise the...' the shipmaster looked uncomfortable, '*other* ship, lord?'

'No!'

Thane practically spat the word. The idea alone was abhorrent.

'When circumstances change, my lord...' said Kale. His wish to recite his Guilliman vied with awareness of his position relative his superhuman Chapter Master. He restricted himself to just that opening line, and a poignant arch of his eyebrow.

'Some circumstances don't change,' said Thane. 'Some walls can never come down.'

'Sir. My lord.'

They both turned. It was Teal.

'I have the Venerable Dreadnought-Marshal Magneric on vox.'

SIX

Vandis System – Mandeville point

The image within the wire hoop of the cable-fed, spring-mounted hololith projector was dark. Had it not been for the drizzle of static and the occasional side-to-side flicker of the shadow shapes within it, then Thane might have concluded that *Excelsior* had lost the signal. The cold blue glow of the frequency-tether bulb confirmed otherwise. Primary power aboard *Obsidian Sky* was out. Even bridge lighting was down.

Illuminated under periodic fountains of sparks, he could make out Magneric. The hard, angular definition of his armour shone like a faceted work of jet. Silver cuneiform picked out the edgework of black, battle-scarred ceramite plates. But this was not the moulded plate of a battle-brother. It was the immense armour housing of a Dreadnought's sarcophagus.

'Do I address *the* Venerable Magneric?' spoke Thane, forgetting for a moment, in his reverence, where he was. 'I studied your actions in the defence of Terra as a neophyte.

The sally that silenced the Fourth Legion's guns is legendary, even if it cost you your life.'

'The Emperor lights our true path!' the Dreadnought thundered, shouting Thane down as he still spoke as though he had not heard, or had listened and deemed it irrelevant. His speakers were pitched to a frightening volume, his words stretched and distorted by the interlink as though delivered through a pipe. 'Not once but twice. Twice!'

The image dissolved into drizzling static and the audio went with it. For a moment, ork gibberish pushed hard onto the line, and then the hololith returned, albeit for several seconds without sound. The Venerable Dreadnought must have been similarly affected by the break in the link but, judging by the flutter of the scriptural parchments that lay over his speakers, he spoke yet.

'Praise be!' the Dreadnought boomed, rising to full volume in a grind of static. 'Praise be!'

Thane turned enquiringly to Teal.

'There's nothing I can do, lord. The interruptions are at their end.'

The command deck shook under a series of escalating blows, and Thane gripped the handrail that encircled the hololith plate. Mass-explosions and slow disintegrations lit the screens of the main viewer as they cycled through shots of the Fists Exemplar fleet. An aegis frigate came apart under a sustained torrent of macro-fire, its hull flaking away like rust. An ork warship vanished in a ball of light. Another lost its shields in a spasm of current, then was engulfed and destroyed. The cruiser *Angel Astra* split down her centre, metal shearing and snapping and spinning into space, coming apart before the ork assault ship that was ploughing into her spine. Light attack craft burst and died, indistinguishable from static.

'Magneric. Magneric!' Static rippled through the loop-array like blast debris in a warpstorm. He waited for a response for as long as he felt he could keep his attention from the needs of his own ship. And then, half-buried in noise, like the blip of an emergency transponder to alert a searching friend that the debris hid survivors, came the voice.

'The Emperor guided us to Dzelenic Four and showed us the way to victory. Seven centuries I pursued the traitor that calls me friend, and it was for a purpose. Praise be!'

It sounded as though that final coda was carried by other voices in the background, but it was impossible to be sure. To add to the orks' interference, there was a disconnect of several seconds between what Thane heard and what he saw. Holding a dialogue with the most considered of Fists Exemplar would have been difficult, but it was abundantly clear that carrying on a conversation with the Venerable Black Templar even under the most ideal of circumstances would have been a challenge.

'Victory, Dreadnought-Marshal?' he urged. 'Victory over the orks? Is that why they pursue you in such numbers, for information that you carry?

'Abhor the witch, deny the witch, destroy the witch!'

Thane tightened his grip over the handrail, hung his head, closed his eyes, and let out an exasperated growl. The shiver of shield-diffused detonations ran through the metal and into his palms.

'Our faith in Him is our armour,' Magneric continued, unabated. 'His divinity is the sword in our hands. Alas for the weakness of my Navigator's faith, his mind was destroyed when the witch craft pulled us from the warp. Loathe the mutant!'

Thane left the hololithic projection to its diatribe. The Black Templars' fundamentalist beliefs were subject to hushed discussion among the Successor Chapters, but were nominally a secret nonetheless. To hear them declared so brazenly by a veteran of the Heresy War made Thane uneasy.

Nonetheless. 'Whatever the Venerable's state of mind, shipmaster, it is clear to me that he has something of value,' he said aside to Kale. 'Anything that the orks work so hard to keep from me is something that I want. Release emergency power to main drive and forward shields. Ram the alien from our path if you must. Divert the necessary power to tractors and teleporters.'

'No!' Magneric's time-delayed static-hiss rumbled from the array like thunder. 'The Emperor protects.'

'I do not understand. You sent out a signal for aid.'

The Dreadnought's bulk pivoted against the enshrouding darkness, turning sufficiently far from his hololith's field of capture to boom something at a crew serf without Thane's hearing. 'I am sending your ship my sarcophagus' vid-log of the battle. May it lift your heart, brother. Use it gloriously.'

Thane looked to Kale, who looked in turn to the vox-liaison, Teal. She frowned. 'Data exload from *Obsidian Sky* confirmed but we've received nothing yet.' A few tense moments passed. 'Wait... Data packet received, not by us, but by the *Interdictor*.'

Thane thumped the handrail. 'Who did he think that he was talking to?'

While he marshalled his frustration, Kale had crossed to the strategium and reformatted the viewer to a split screen. Individual screens on the left-hand side continued to flick between shots of the Fists Exemplar fleet.

The frigate picket was coming apart under an intolerable weight of firepower. The *Dauntless*, *Champion* and *Noble Savage* were destroyed. The *Grey Ranger* was burning, backup generators spitting emergency power into space.

The right-side screens had been combined to run a single, near-real-time feed of the second Black Templar crusade group, crudely overlain by a black grid showing the divides between the screens. They were barely moving at all now, held up in a mass of ork warships. *Dantalion* and her accompanying cruisers were just sliding into field, enveloped in an oil-on-water pattern of void-shield discharge as the three massive ships sailed into the orks' heaviest ordnance. Arriving from the opposite direction, the ork carrier crunched into the rear of its escort fleet, spitting out a volume of fire equivalent to an entire Navy battlegroup, weird power squirming over its ramshackle sail. Another black cruiser blossomed into fire. From the vid-feed alone, Thane could not be sure that it was not the *Interdictor*.

'Zerberyn gets himself into the right place at the right time once again. Can we get a message to him?'

'No, lord. The carrier's blanket denial broadcast grows exponentially more severe as you approach.'

'Do we have any ships unengaged?'

'*Paragon* is more-or-less intact and has drive power

restored.' Kale consulted a display. 'And *Excelsior* and her escorts.'

'Transmit new orders to those ships. Intercept *Dantalion* with orders to escort *Interdictor* from the battle and prepare for immediate translation: return to Terra with all speed, it is nearer than Phall, and hope that Magneric carries information of worth. Dispatch *Guilliman* to accompany them.'

'Respectfully, lord, she's the second most powerful ship in the fleet.'

'I expect a degree of insubordination from my First Captain, shipmaster, I do not expect it from you.'

The old shipmaster clipped his heels. 'Aye, lord.'

'Use it gloriously, brother,' came Magneric's voice through the distortion. 'Praise be.'

'Hold firm, Dreadnought-Marshal. Your brother, Bohemond, saved my Chapter from my stubbornness on Eidolica and you can expect the same today. Whether the Emperor wishes it or no. Magneric? Magneric!'

The projector emitted an angry hiss. A whiff of ozone. Gabbling voices. The detector picked up the orks' gibberish frequencies and reconstituted the random noise in eerie repeat patterns and oscillating waves.

The link had been severed.

They had lost Magneric.

SEVEN

Vandis

The lighting on the command deck of *Obsidian Sky* plinked on and off, on and off. Half-second flashes of artificial light slid across machine-smooth black metal and the stiff, liveried corpses that lay across them. Plastek console frames stuffed with broken glass flashed back, each jagged piece a lens showing a reflected snapshot of a dead ship. Coolant gases spumed into the chamber from a damaged radiator assembly in the ceiling, filling the area with a vaporous, sub-zero froth.

At the aft section there was a raised platform, above which flew a white banner bearing the Sigismund cross and a blood splatter in the lower left corner. It was ringed with displays and terminals, all dead. Castellan Ralstan had taken an exploding oxygen pipe in the face. He lay on his front on the steps down to the main bridge, armour cracked and burned, arm drawn up as if to conceal the ruin of his head. Light and shadow came and passed: on, off. Shipmaster Ericus was fetched up against the aft bulkhead as though someone had shoved him against it and put a bullet through his forehead.

Down a level, into the main deck, the bodies lay more thickly. Some had been crushed under falling panels or buried under shattered glass, and now lay staring up like dead men frozen under thin ice. They had been electrocuted, burned, cut by glass shrapnel and bludgeoned by high-mass debris, most while still strapped into work station chairs. One had been reduced to a carbonaceous smear on the seat leather by a catastrophic overload of his auspex. The console was still sputtering, sparking and fizzing into the nitrogen mist.

'Boarding torpedoes incoming,' mumbled the Master Ordinatum, Franzek, as though drawing each word one at a time from his head. Blood matted his hair and ran down the side of his neck. His eyes were glazed. The harsh lighting intermittently exposed his blanched face. On, off. On, off. 'I've never seen so many at once.'

'Faith is the first victim of thought. Keep firing,' Magneric answered with a metallic rumble, stepping back from the hissing hololith projector.

Dead too.

'Firing... aye.'

Targeting grids were dead. Auto-loaders were dead.

The gunnery chief was arming whatever had been already loaded and launching it manually, as fast as his shell-shocked nervous system could still manage. Each shot sent a shudder through the ship, a nail recoil-driven into the hull. Inertial stabilisers were dead too, but the crew, what remained of it, no longer even recognised the shaking. By sheer mass, Magneric stood immovably in the middle of the command dais.

'We deny the alien this ship, until the Emperor gives us our leave to rest.'

'*Ave Imperator*,' they replied.

It was inconceivable that *Obsidian Sky* could destroy every last torpedo, but they could thin their numbers. And miracles happened, Magneric knew. The hull squealed in torment, shaken, this time from without, as though being attacked with a drill.

'We shall know no fear!'

With a sudden lurch, the drilling stopped. Seconds elapsed without an explosion. The crew held their breath, and held onto their brace positions. They knew what a torpedo hit felt like.

'Sound the general alert,' boomed Magneric.

'Aye.'

The bondsman covering at the main drive station – Cecillia – staggered from starboard to port, thumbed open a transparent plastek cover to expose a red key in a slot, and then turned it. The flickering light was immediately shot through with red. The effect was bitty, hazard-striping the debris-strewn deck as dull red lights glowed from broken screens.

Internal sensors were dead. Communications were dead.

Without them, necessity had demanded the command crew be creative. Power utilisation profiles indicated active terminals in all sections. Oxygen saturations pinpointed signs of life at muster points on all decks. Kaplin, at Operations, had breathlessly suggested retrofitting a pair of servitors to link up as a two-way communicator, but there had been no time to implement it. Now, Kaplin was directing that reckless enthusiasm into the pump action of a Mk IX shotgun. He took position on the steps near the late castellan, a slightly crazed look in his eyes.

Magneric stamped through an about-face. The assault cannon mounted on his right shoulder ran through a sequence of test cycles. His immense power fist rotated, clicked and reversed, like some kind of puzzle clock. He trained the spinning gun barrel onto the magnetically locked blast doors that sealed off the command deck from the rest of the ship.

He could almost *feel* the xenos aboard his ship, the way a man of flesh and bone would feel the tasteless, textureless, odourless itch of a radiation dose. This new breed of greenskin was a dangerous foe. They fought tactically, acted coherently: if they had forces to spare to claim his crippled ship then he could only assume they would do so exactly as he would in their place. The command deck would be the priority target. Then the enginarium, gunnery control, the flight bays.

It was useful however to remind oneself that they were not men. They were still orks.

'Rolans,' he voxed, attempting to raise the battle-brother barracked in the deck below with a squad of Black Templars and two platoons of armsmen serfs. 'Sword Brother?'

A light crackle of static filled his acoustic register.

The carrier had somehow managed to kill off helm-to-helm vox. Until then, Magneric had thought that unblockable.

Cold gases swirled. The lights rattled, and blinked. On, off. On, off.

On...

Time stretched, bloated. The blast doors seemed suddenly a yawning distance away, although his own triple-grid spatial positioning system insisted that their relative positions were unchanged. It was as if, in this chamber alone, the laws of the universe had been relaxed, the space between particles expanding even as the particles themselves remained exactly as they were. Making room.

Off.

There was a pop, like a broken vacuum seal, and an ork burst out of the vapour cloud as if it had been hidden there all along and slammed into the middle of the main deck. The flickering light made the sudden appearance of its gruesome mass even more unreal. It was the monster that stalked the unevolved lobes of the human brain, fear centres unchanged since *Homo sapiens sapiens* first emerged from the forests and onto the plains of prehistoric Terra. And now, two hundred millennia and half a segmentum removed, they still recognised a beast.

The ork bared yellow fangs and roared.

Kaplin roared back, mad with horror, and swung about, leading with his shotgun. There was a boom. Scatter shot from both barrels tore up the ork's black-and-white body armour and riddled its heavy jaw with pellets. It bullied through, tusked mouth wide like a dog thirsty for the rain.

Feet spread and mag-locked to the deck, Magneric's torso swung one hundred and eighty degrees and obliterated the ork's skull with a point-four-second burst of fire. Exit wounds and ricochets wasted the surrounding consoles, but the wellbeing of his ship was no longer a priority. Better to deny it to the alien.

'Deny the alien! Kill the alien!'

More orks charged through the mist and onto the command deck, and by the strobing light men began to die.

An axe split Franzek's head like a gourd before the dazed man even realised he was in danger. Seated beside him, Merrel punched his belt release buckle and rose, drawing his side-arm. A thunderblast from a brick-like stubber dropped him back down, printing the ruined contents of his chest over the console. The ork belted its pistol, hauled Merrel's remains from the station and, leaving its axe where it was buried in Franzek's head, stabbed a wedge-like device with a blinking base into the unit. The surviving screens immediately went haywire. Cecillia was ripped, chair fittings and all, from the main drive station and hurled screaming across the chamber. Her body broke so hard against the stainless steel aquila mounted over the prow in place of a viewscreen that she put a dent in its wing. Flinching from the meat-slap sound, Kaplin screamed a homily ad-libbed with wild obscenities and nonsense as he backed up the steps. He pumped his shotgun, spitting out a pair of spent casings, and then fired, whizzing the air with shrapnel and exploding a lumen fitting in the ceiling.

They were outmuscled, outgunned. The bondsmen of the Black Templars had never been so outclassed.

Venerable Magneric advanced at a measured pace, stitching the air with short, ultra-precise bursts of assault cannon fire. He shredded an ork in identical, almost uniform checker-pattern body armour with a point-three-second salvo, then pivoted, tracked, *locked* – and fired. A point-seven-second burst chewed through armour and skin and riddled the main drive terminal with bone.

With an implosive clap of displacement, an ork teleported directly into his path.

Magneric did not know what manner of thoughts filled the mind of an ork. Words? Images? A deep, ancestral dream of destruction and slaughter? He had never considered it. He regretted that failing now, for whatever the creature had expected to encounter when it had stepped into its ship's teleportation portal, a Black Templars Dreadnought in the throes of battle rage had not been one of them.

The expression on its beast face was beyond price.

Magneric's power fist punched into the ork's chest and lifted it from the deck like an eel on a spear. Concentric rings of adamantium teeth spun in opposing directions like propellers, blending the ork in its entirety and spraying its vaporised remains.

The remaining orks took cover in pits and behind bulkheads, and fired back with noisy bursts of stubber-fire.

Keeping low, Kaplin ran to Merrel's blood-sprayed terminal and took cover behind the dead bondsman's chair. He tugged at the blinking spike that the ork had left embedded in it. He could not move it a millimetre.

'Some kind of denial shunt,' he yelled, ducking onto his haunches behind Merrel's chair as bullets flew overhead. 'It's opened the outer doors to the flight bays and disengaged the cohesion fields.'

Torpedoes. Assault boats. Teleport commandos. An assault on all fronts, coordinated, and with overwhelming force. Magneric despised his enemy enough to be impressed.

Obsidian Sky was not like the ships of his former VII

Legion brothers. A vessel like the Fists Exemplar flagship was a mobile fortress, constructed for the projection of force and the holding of territory. *Obsidian Sky* was not built to be defended. She was a blade, a tool of incision and conquest.

Stubber-rounds spanking off his metal skin, Magneric launched a full spread of grenades from his power fist's underslung launchers. Primed for airburst, the withering frag-storm blew the orks' improvised shelter open. The survivors, black-and-white bodyplate glittering with fragmentation shards, he mowed down with an almost hot-blooded relish.

It was moments like these when it still felt good to be alive.

His assault cannon wound down with a squeal, nitrogen condensate hissing to vapour on contact.

'Um.' Kaplin stared mutely at the console beside his. 'Shipmaster Attonax of the *Palimodes* has been trying to raise us, Dreadnought-Marshal. They... express their intent to depart with the Fists Exemplar.'

Pistons in the back of Magneric's legs retracted with a hydraulic wheeze, and tilted him back to face the ceiling. What remained of his flesh body after the fall of Tranquility Wall floated in an amniotic sac deep within the metal behemoth that interred him. For centuries, fury alone had driven him on. It was a living thing, that fury, in a way that he no longer was, pure and unsullied. Immortal. Others granted the highest honour of service beyond death required prolonged periods of rest between deployments, but not him. His rage denied him. He had retained his rank. He had retained his name. His fury too had a name: Kalkator. But now it seemed that it had no further to take him.

'You seek to escape me at the last, Kalkator? By the Emperor's decree, never! As we agreed, traitor, we escape together or we die together.'

His chassis pivoted towards Kaplin. 'Status of engines?' he demanded.

Kaplin swallowed and hurriedly picked his way through the debris to the main drive station. It took him a moment to interpret the unfamiliar read-outs. 'Partial thrusters only.'

Magneric's mind retreated to the cold space, that particular aggregation of cyborganic interfaces where his sarcophagus' inscrutable machine-spirit met the quiet luminosity of his own immortal soul. The place where the Emperor breathed His will into his interred remains and gave them not just life, but spirit.

'It will suffice. Set a collison course for the ork carrier and fire thrusters.'

'Sir?'

'Are my speakers impaired?'

'No, venerable lord,' Kaplin answered crisply, setting down his shotgun to prod the new coordinates into the unfamiliar set of controls. An urgently blinking light back at the communications station caught his eye. He leaned across. 'It's the *Palimodes* again, I think.'

'Ignore it. Forwards. Always forwards. Let the fireball destroy us all!'

'Aye, sir.'

'Then–'

Magneric turned back to the blast doors.

He could hear weapons fire. Not the dispersive blooms of the armsmen's shotguns, nor the explosive noise-makers of the orks. It was the focused double-blasts of mass-reactive rounds.

Space Marines.

With a pneumatic hiss the blast doors slid open. The ten-centimetre-thick insulated barrier removed, the frozen air filled with the roar of bolter fire. Two Black Templars, firing from the hip, were covering each other's withdrawal down the long corridor towards the command deck. At the far end, a mob of orks in neat black-and-white checked plate and horned helms advanced behind a bank of massive shields fitted with eye slits and what looked like heavy flamers.

The auto-defence turrets were dead.

The Space Marines' shots blazed across the rank of shields. There was a deep-chested *huck*, like a cleared throat, and a launched grenade flew over the shield wall and went off under the Black Templar currently providing overwatch. The explosion peeled away his power armour and slammed him, broken, into the bulkhead. His comrade was thrown flat, but immediately pulled himself up on his elbows to rake the shield line on full-auto. The orks pushed on, impervious to anything lighter than a heavy bolter.

Their slow advance revealed, squatting on the deck behind them, an abhorrence almost reminiscent of a orkish tech-priest. Except that was impossible.

The orks had always possessed a native affinity for low technology, but nothing as specialised as this. The alien adept sat within a hulking ring of bodyguards, beside a maintenance hatch that it had clearly just blasted open using the plasma cutter grafted to its left arm. The panel's internal controls were connected to a slate-like device in the ork's hands and by a set of jump leads to the enormous power pack on its back. But even that abomination lost all power to offend beside the giant standing over it as a man would stand beside a dog.

Its brute size and vibrating, piston-driven fighting suit were impressive, but what struck Magneric at once was the realisation that the white and black plates bolted on as a dermal layer were ceramite. It was Adeptus Astartes power armour. Crusade Armour. Mark II. Magneric recognised the colours and the emblem that stamped them, though he doubted whether anyone who had not lived through those times now would.

White and black. Like the orks in the command deck. Like these orks here. Likely, it was the progenitor design, a scheme that the orks had come to associate with power and strength.

Luna Wolves.

Magneric could think of only one world upon which an ork could have come upon so infamous a relic.

With a battle cry last heard in the flesh at the gates of Holy Terra booming from his speakers, Magneric stamped forward, blocking the blast doors with his armoured bulk.

'I am Magneric of the Black Templars. I denied the Palace of my God to His wayward sons. I deny it to you, xenos.'

A torrent of assault cannon fire chewed across the orks' shields and drove them back.

'Magneric denies you! Kaplin! Fire thrusters!'

EIGHT

Vandis

Gloriously unrefined firepower unfolded about *Alcazar Remembered* like butterfly wings, carving open ork ships, murdering their shields and leaving them to perish in her wake in puffs of fire. She had the look of an angel, but she was a gladiator. The void was her arena. The frigates *Chastened* and *Unbroken* were the first to shoot through in her wake. Explosions lit the debris field; lance beams and fighter contrails, shield flares and shelling.

The orks' mass carrier pivoted its main gun.

It was a huge bronzed barrel the length of a capital ship, fed with masses of brightening plasma coils and finned by that sail-like radiator array. With a flash of energised plasma it fired.

Thane's data-display screamed an alert as an immense gravity spike crunched through *Unbroken*. The command deck shook, like a bomb shelter under sustained shelling. It was smoke and klaxons, shouts, squeals of metal pushed to the limits of tolerance. The main viewer crackled with static, showing ships and ordnance and flying debris screwing off-course and spraying out in all directions. *Dutiful* was snatched in by the pull of *Unbroken*'s suddenly swollen mass and slingshotted back. Following in on maximum drive, there was nothing that the cruiser *Bastion of Arete* could do to avoid her. Destruction was instantaneous and total.

'Starboard void banks nearing saturation,' said Weylon Kale, not shouting – never shouting – but terminally close. His voice was hoarse from breathing smoke and his eyes were raw. The old shipmaster had slotted in at the strategium to replace the section liaison, who lay spread out on the deck under a fire blanket, only hands and third-degree burns showing.

'Increasing capacity with backup generators,' the serf beside him screamed back.

Kale turned to Thane.

'They'll hold a few minutes more, but against a shot from that...'

'The Fists Exemplar do not leave their own behind.'

'My lord, at what cost?'

Thane stood tall as the deck around him trembled. It was a sense of duty, the stubborn grit that was so much a part of him, that stayed his course. Could anyone but a son of Dorn feel that overriding sense of obligation that the gene-seed of their primarch-progenitor imparted? The noble Ultramarines? The Dark Angels? Could they even understand it?

Thane doubted it. He *doubted* it.

'We are the Last Wall. There is no further to fall back.'

'Still no response from *Obsidian Sky*,' said Teal, voice

wavering up and down with the hits to the shields and the shaking of the deck.

'Keep sending.'

'Aye. Lord, the Iron Warriors ship, *Palimodes*, is signalling. They're expressing their... gratitude.'

Thane gripped a little more fiercely to the handrail than the shaking of the command deck made necessary. 'Acknowledge it. Order them to decelerate and come about on our heading. They can draw some of the fire off our flanks while we move in to recover the *Obsidian Sky*.'

The subaltern keyed in the message and hit transmit. There was a tense pause.

'Response,' snapped Teal. Her face went pale, her eyes moving as though scanning a large block of text. She swallowed. 'They respectfully say no.'

'No?'

'The essence of it, lord.'

Thane mastered the tic of annoyance that threatened to break the resolute set of his jaw. 'Then let them go. Any word from Zerberyn?'

'No, lord, but Auspectoria reports *Dantalion* and a number of vessels breaking off and heading for the Mandeville point.'

'Chapter Master. Come and take a look at this.' Kale called Thane over to the strategium and directed his attention to the analytics at his station screen. The information was similar to that displayed in hololith over the chart desk, but more readily formatted into digestible data-scales, while the two-dimensional output was easier on unaugmented eyes. As of right then, it showed a fuzzy black cross surrounded by

ship debris and power signatures denotive of bording torpedoes, updated every few seconds by a sonar-like sweep
of code. 'We're approaching *Obsidian Sky*.'

'Good. Now get these orks off my viewscreen and show
me.'

The viewer blinked from split-screen to a single image
of the bloated mass carrier. The sweep of its upper and aft
sections were edged red, the sun eclipsed, its dark side lit
by the fires and weapon lights of the dwarfed capital-class
ships in its shadow. From the speed and angle of drift, it
was clear that the image was unaugmented real-time. Rolling with the hits to his shields, Thane made his way back
to the command throne and punched up a magnification
of *Obsidian Sky*.

The screen changed, zoomed, and suddenly there she
was, gliding like a disguised backhand knife under the carrier's side. Collision course.

'Raise Magneric,' Thane roared, voice-amplification pushing maximum and whining with feedback. 'Now!'

'No response,' Teal cried back.

'Cut power to main drive. Thrusters, full reverse.'

Wordlessly, Kale carried out the command, liver-spotted
old hands fluttering over the array of controls. Thane felt
a g-force surge run through the already straining ship, but
it was too late.

Not with all the legendary stubbornness of Rogal Dorn
himself could he fail to see what was to come next.

The carrier had left the Black Templars vessel for dead
until then, content to dispatch boarding torpedoes and
assault pods, but now the few dozen kilometres between

them erupted into a lava stream of shells and explosive rounds. The two ships were already too close together for primary weapons, but even under that restriction the volume of fire that the ork's command ship was capable of putting out was staggering. *Obsidian Sky*'s armoured prow simply dissolved, as if the ork ship were projecting an energy field that was causing it to dematerialise on contact. But *Obsidian Sky* was just too much ship, even for the mass carrier, to completely obliterate with defence batteries alone.

The space narrowed to under a kilometre.

Her bow had been burned to a flat stump. There was a cauterising flare as ship met shields.

'Venerable...' Thane breathed.

With sublime slowness, *Obsidian Sky* plunged into the carrier's port side.

It was not slow. Thane knew that. But the scales and distances involved made a nonsense of any human notion of speed. The shorn, void-exposed inner bulkheads of *Obsidian Sky*'s forward section were folded in and crushed, driven deeper into the carrier's crust by failing thrusters. Her hull began to deform, ripples spreading back as her starboard thruster blew out. Drive plasma flaring out into space, *Obsidian Sky* tilted, ground in, and then finally crashed sideways into the larger ship.

Thane winced from the first spark of the explosion, a pure white nucleus of destructive energy swelling up from *Obsidian Sky*'s drive core. It lasted a fraction of a second, then rushed out in a flash that washed the entire viewscreen white. As if to compensate for the glare, deck lighting dipped. Terminals surged, arced and blew out in serial cascades of sparks. The blast front hit seconds behind the electromagnetic surge, and slammed Thane back into the command throne.

Shaking his head clear of shield saturation alerts and the low whine of decompression warnings, Thane reached up for the command throne's grip studs and pulled himself back up. His multi-lung took over his breathing as his chest filled with smoke and his blood acidity spiked. He felt the sudden burn of frustrated anger. They could still have seen the *Obsidian Sky* and her crew clear; instead Magneric had almost destroyed them all.

'Report,' he called out, but everyone was still pulling themselves together or nursing flickering consoles like primitives around a fire.

A pair of serfs at auspectoria hurriedly shared notes and drew some quick adjustments to the pattern of curves and vectors on the scanner table. At the same time, the main viewer began to clear and a rough cheer went up from the command crew. The mass carrier was listing, a massive hole blasted out of its side. It was possible to make out distinct decks within the almost perfect hemispherical cutaway, lights twinkling behind the debris cloud and coherence fields like stars within a nebula.

'*Obsidian Sky* is down,' reported an auspex serf. 'Two Black Templars ships still intact. Cruisers. One of them is the *Interdictor*. *Dantalion, Bulwark,* and *Faceless Warrior* are with them.'

'The ork ships, my lord,' said Kale, the swirling colours of the strategium chart desk like racing storm clouds across his face. 'They're assuming new headings, moving off from the carrier.'

Thane sank back into the command throne and summoned a pared-back copy of the strategium read-outs to his data-display. The orks were disengaging, breaking for the system perimeter. But why? Why run? Even with their leviathan flagship crippled they had the Imperial forces grossly outgunned.

'I am seeing some unusual immaterial extrusions centred around the ork carrier,' Thane said.

'Teleporter activity,' Kale explained. 'High volume over short distances.'

'It is unlike orks to evacuate. Or to run.'

'This leadership caste we've been hearing about?'

Thane cupped his chin in his hand as the deck around him shook. But why run?

The movement in the viewer was so subtle that it took even Thane's sharpened senses a moment to pick it up. The carrier's fin-like primary weapon was cleaving through the wreckage field. Thane saw coils charging, energy gathering in glowing capacitors along the massive cannon's length. For a moment, he was looking straight down its barrel. *Alcazar Remembered* was too big to move out of the way. Anything else was a stubborn act of futility.

An ember struck up within the splayed bore of the cannon, vibrating, caged within a magnetic field. Coming from within that debris cloud it looked more like a birthing sun than a weapon. Thane saw a glint, the tip of the sunbeam that lanced towards him, then it blinked like a shooting star as the beam shot across the bows.

A miss. Thane eased his grip on the armrests and let out a breath. In their panic, the orks had wasted their shot. That was his first instinct, based neither on evidence nor on past experience, and as such he was unusually loath to relinquish it, even once it became clear that the carrier wasn't cutting off the beam. In fact, it was intensifying.

Vandis.

At first, the red giant seemed to shrug off the beam boring into its surface, but after a few seconds, a dark sunspot began to form around the drill site. Bubbles of core matter broke the surface as the sunspot began to *sink*. It became a blister, then a bruise, a black canker that bored deeper into its parent body and pulled more stellar matter in. The bottomless black of its event horizon garnered a halo, brilliant, burning white.

The accretion disc of a black hole.

Thane slowly rose, watching with a very raw, very *human* awe. The orks had transformed one of the most stable and intransigent forces in the universe into a weapon, and simply to keep Magneric's information from reaching Terra they were using it to demolish a star.

A star!

What could any man – even an angel of death – do in the face of such reckless power?

The carrier itself, the most massive ship by far, was the first to feel the effects. Already backsliding, it stopped firing as its cannon was yanked out of alignment, and then slowly bent. In its shadow were two more Black Templars cruisers that had been disabled and seized by grapnels rather than destroyed. Drifting and helpless, they began to come apart. Hull plates crunched, compacted down, atmosphere squirting out as hardpoints tore loose and spun away to be devoured by infinity. *Chastened*, just sliding into tractor range, drove her reverse engines to maximum and just about managed to remain still. She came about in order to bring her main drive to bear. Thane saw what her shipmaster was trying to do, but manoeuvring thrusters couldn't compete with the black hole's pull and she was dragged, side-on, until gravity overwhelmed structural integrity and she blew in a hideously compact explosion.

A shuddering groan passed through *Alcazar Remembered.*

She was more powerful than her frigate escorts, more than the Black Templars cruisers, but she was also larger, more susceptible to the gravity waves lashing at her hull. Each shudder came with a bang, as though the bulkheads were having their rivets pulled and then being physically snapped. A barrage of high-intensity radiation blinded the viewscreen and killed shipboard communications.

'Full reverse!' Thane roared, a string of bolts bursting along a seam from the bulkhead behind him on a scream of inrushing air. 'All hands prepare for emergency translation! Get us out of here now!'

NINE

Terra – the Imperial Palace

Vangorich knew that his rivals on the Senatorum, and even some of his friends, such that he possessed, had his apartments under surveillance. In recent days it had come to the point where there was rarely a moment in which the agents of two or more lords wouldn't pass each other on the street. The increasingly erratic behaviour of the likes of Mesring and Zeck had exacerbated matters. The staged attempt on Veritus' life had certainly not helped.

Even at this early hour, the artificial twilight of the Palace was thronged, the sun as removed from the reality of these people's own small lives as the love of the God-Emperor of Man.

There was the catering shift bound for the Imperial Fleet College of Strategy, extravagant in pressed white shirts and black tails. Talking quietly amongst themselves, they paused just outside the gated compound while one of their number crossed the street to buy a pack of lhos from the kiosk. Then there was the pretty young girl – fifteen, maybe sixteen – selling soap and devotionals from a stand beneath a humming bronze extractor unit. She smiled pleasantly, chatting to the workers gathered with their bowls under the electrical warmth. There was the street confessor, the work detail that had been picketed on top of the deactivated transformer substation for the better part of a week, the two-man unit assigned to the corner by the Adeptus Arbites to pre-empt that particular 'flashpoint', the scrivener hawking his services, the servitor detail carting steel barrels of imported water for the Administratum silo in the neighbouring ward. By comparison, the street sweep working around the Navy men's feet was a little obvious, if only because it was such a classic.

And if nothing else, Vangorich appreciated vintage.

That was not to say there were not times when an out-of-the-way office deep in the labyrinthine quiet of the Inner Wards was appealing, but it generally suited him to be seen where tradition expected the Grand Master of the Officio Assassinorum to be. It kept everybody honest, and prevented misunderstandings.

And so it was that the appearance at the gate of a man of medium height, medium build, and middle years caused more of a stir than so nondescript an individual might rationally expect to generate.

Vangorich was happy enough to let those agents make their reports. Partly because it would be a phenomenal waste of energy to stop them all, but primarily because at the time that his body double was deactivating the security system, he was sitting quite comfortably in the eighth level suite of a fortified tower overlooking Bastion Ledge, several lines of latitude away. The armourglass window offered a limited view of the Water Gardens and of the sunrise over the Imperial Palace. At least two-thirds of the offering, however, was taken by the automatic weapons arrays, surveillance jammers, and psychic null-generators that cloaked the compound. The Inquisition was commendably zero-tolerance in their attitude to security.

'Some wine?' he asked, leaning across the low-slung reception table and proffering the bottle.

'Thank you, sir, no,' said Krule, raising his hand. 'Never while I'm plotting.'

Vangorich smiled and reset the bottle on the table.

It had a yellowing label inscribed in a curling script too obtuse for Vangorich to make out. He doubted it was actually Terran, but it looked old. Rigil Kentaurus perhaps, or Prospero. The Inquisitorial Representative's suite had suffered a reversion to the minimalist since Wienand's brief departure. The soft furnishings had been retired, or rearranged for more efficient effect. The priceless artworks and artefacts that had adorned the walls and tabletops were now warehoused in whatever vast silo the Inquisition must employ for such purposes. It was remarkable what a cull at the top could accomplish.

He took a sip from his glass.

Fruity. Woody. It smelled floral, the way he imagined a functioning ecosystem must smell.

'Where were we?'

'Mars, sir.'

Vangorich knew that, of course. He had an eidetic memory, a product of extensive training and cognitive therapies,

and of certain genetic gifts. The same could have been achieved with implants, but they had their own drawbacks. Keeping track of the byzantine comings and goings of the Officio was not a simple matter of memory capacity in any case. It needed a human touch.

'How many operatives do we still have there?'

Krule picked up a slate from the several spread over the table between them.

'Red Haven cadre. Saskine Haast of Temple Vindicare. Mariazet Isolde of Temple Callidus. Clementina Yendl of Temple Vanus. Tybalt of Temple Eversor. And Raznick of the Inquisition if you choose to count him as one of ours.' He read on a way. 'It looks like Yendl had managed to cultivate a useful resource on the Mechanicus' project to replicate the orks' teleportation technology, before she lost contact. We're assuming the worst, I presume?'

'The official line from his supervisor is "reassigned". Yendl's looking into it, but it's not the end of the world. Her pride is a little scratched, but there are other avenues of investigation under way.'

'Translating a planet,' said Krule, lowering the slate and gazing out of the window. 'Damn, that would be a thing to see.'

'The trial data is all in Yendl's intelligence log. The so-called Grand Experiment is proving as much a dead end for Kubik as it is for us.'

'But if it could be made to work...'

Krule let the implications hang. They were so encompassing, so fundamental, that it was difficult to take the necessary step back to see them. Assimilation of the orks' propulsion technology would strike at the very pillars of Imperial stability. With such a power, the Mechanicus would be able to move anything, anywhere. The Adeptus Astronomica would be no more, the Navis Nobilite cast down at best and persecuted by a vengeful Inquisition at worst. The fleets of Mars would render the Navy and the Chartists obsolete at a stroke.

Schism. On a scale not seen since the Age of Strife.

Vangorich nodded darkly.

'Merely pointing out, sir,' said Krule, breaking the sombre mood, 'if this intelligence log were somehow to find its way onto Sark or Gibran's desk then you'd have all the Senatorum backing you could want to take Kubik's head.'

'If it comes to it, but safer to keep something so inflammatory to ourselves if possible. I gather that Haast and Isolde have managed to successfully integrate into Kubik's household on Mars. What about when he is here on Terra – habits, and so on?'

Krule picked up another report from the stack.

'A creature of routine, as you'd expect. Getting to him shouldn't be an issue. The problem would be the windows available. He doesn't seem to sleep, keeps to public places by and large, and he's always accompanied.' He shrugged, apologetic. 'They don't give much consideration to privacy.'

'What about when he travels?'

'Mechanicus lighter operating out of Daylight space port. The Mechanicus provides their own pilots and ground crew as well as a skitarii cohort. Knowing the Mechanicus, it's probably better armed than it looks.'

Vangorich conceded that with a slight tip of his glass.

'Just how formidable is the Fabricator General, assuming that an example needed to be made?'

'Assuming?' Krule sat back, crossing his muscular arms behind his head along the back of the low couch, as comfortable in someone else's private space as only a man his size could be. 'I could take him.'

'Have you ever killed one of the Mechanicus?'

'You'd know if I had, sir.'

Vangorich smiled.

'Have *you*, sir?' Krule asked.

Vangorich considered a moment. No one else would have dared ask their Grand Master such a question. It mooted the possibility that 'no' could be an answer. Another person might have raised it privately out of concern for Vangorich's professional competence, but not Beast. He knew better.

'No,' he admitted.

'Do you want me to set things in motion?'

Vangorich took a deep breath and shook his head, staring at the slush pile of slates, info-logs, and reports. Selecting a member of the Senatorum Imperialis who had acted with sufficiently witless culpability to warrant death was not difficult. It was, to borrow his favourite Navy aphorism, like launching a torpedo and hitting space. No, the challenge, the surgical *art*, was to identify that member whose untimely removal would most effect improvement in the rest.

He released the breath. Slowly. Deliberately. He massaged the stiffness from his neck.

'Udo,' he said after a few seconds. 'Tell me about the Lord Commander.'

Krule rummaged for the relevant slate just as a minor earth tremor rattled the pile on the table. Only Vangorich's cat-like reflexes spared the Inquisition's carpet a wine stain. The hivequake lingered for a few seconds, and then passed. Vangorich transferred his glass to the other hand and lapped wine from his wrist, then stood and moved to the window. An orange glare lit his face. A hab-block was falling away from the Palace skyline, gutted by the ignited gases that were spraying from its exposed, ancient piping. Even through the reinforced armourglass, Vangorich could hear screaming. The long, hapless whine of tocsins spread slowly across the Imperial Palace.

Something had to be done.

He turned to find Krule checking a security alert on his wrist chrono. Krule silenced the audio sounder, then drew a bulky plasma pistol from the concealed holster inside his jacket. He rose quickly and quietly from his chair, gestured to Vangorich to take cover behind the table, and moved out of line from the door, pistol raised and trained.

Doing as he was bidden, Vangorich dropped onto one knee.

He hooked one arm over the table, partially to shelter his face behind it if need be, and pulled the silenced, slender-barrelled hellpistol he carried from his boot. He took aim at the door and glanced at the access panel on the wall beside it. An amber light was pulsing across the display, left to right and occasionally spiking in the middle, like a heart rate monitor. An intruder should have triggered a red alarm. Amber meant that someone with Inquisitorial clearance had entered the suite, effectively placing the automatic weapon turrets and intruder denial systems built into every staircase and corner space into a temporary 'standby' posture. Vangorich's office had all the specifications. The intruder had ninety seconds to provide the correct form of physical identification and the required codes to one of those access panels before things started to get anxious.

The panel display turned to green and flatlined.

Vangorich cleared his mind, stilled his heart. His field of view became the doorframe.

There were, as his own interest in the matter proved, plenty of individuals on Terra with the motive and means to rid themselves of the Grand Master of the Officio Assassinorum. Vangorich doubted there was a security system built that the adepts of the Mechanicus could not break. Lansung and Verreault undoubtedly commanded personnel with the skill set required to break a triple-aquila-rated secure facility, but neither struck Vangorich as desperate enough to try. The Ecclesiarchy, too, maintained a cadre of highly trained and conditioned operatives, and against the warp-touched abilities of the Navis Nobilite and the Imperium's sanctioned psykers, even the Inquisition's defences would come out second best as often as not.

Were any of them the match of Beast Krule?

Vangorich doubted it.

The door handle dropped with a click, and the door swung open.

Vangorich eased himself a little lower against the table and relaxed into the trigger. He angled his body for a head-shot. Unless they were really, *really* good, he would get at least one shot.

As it turned out, he didn't.

With a hiss of air cyclers and magnetised joint hydraulics, Veritus strode through the open door. He came with a waft of cinnamon-scented oils and a hint – a disguised nasal sting – of preservatives. His cream-coloured power armour blinked with indicator lights and protective runes; it had been rubbed down with powdered silver and fluttered with freshly transcribed papyri. The Inquisitorial Representative's mummified face managed to express enough surprise to stay Vangorich's hand.

'Drakan? What are you doing in my apartments?' Veritus' voice was a dry wheeze, like a legacy recording from a scrivener-cherub left to decay over a thousand years of storage.

Vangorich lowered his pistol to the table and stood as the door slid smoothly shut behind the inquisitor. He shrugged.

'It is the most secure location on Terra.'

'So my aides were at pains to point out to me.'

'If it helps, I was informed equally reliably that you'd not be returning from the Inquisitorial Fortress until tomorrow. An attack moon in orbit is just one more excuse for a slip in standards, isn't it?'

Veritus smiled slightly, an odd, grisly re-interpretation of human amusement. He looked tired, Vangorich realised. More worn out than he had ever seen him. It was as if the Inquisitorial Representative had merely dropped by his suite with no grander intention than a few stolen hours of peace and quiet.

Vangorich wondered if he still wore that armour, even when he thought he was alone.

'You are slipping, Drakan,' said Veritus. 'Udin Macht Udo convened an emergency meeting of the High Twelve last night.'

'He did what?'

Veritus glanced sideways at Krule. The Assassin had lowered his plasma pistol, but only marginally.

'Have him put it away, Drakan. You have my assurance that I could do it for him just as easily.'

Krule raised an eyebrow, but nevertheless stowed and reconcealed his weapon at Vangorich's nod.

'Shall I leave you, sir?'

'Thank you, Krule.'

Veritus peered down over the lip of his high gorget collar as Beast Krule moved past him and ducked out. Again the door slid shut and clamped. The hiss of air breathed against the inquisitor's brittle lashes. His expression was unreadable.

'The Lord Commander proposed a motion to suspend the Inquisition from the High Twelve.'

'He did *what*? Has he completely lost his mind?'

'Perhaps. But for once, leveller heads prevailed. Only Tobris Ekharth and Mesring backed it.'

'The Ecclesiarchy I could almost understand supporting a move like that, but Ekharth?' Vangorich swore. 'Does that man even have a nervous system of his own?'

'The Lord Commander was most aggrieved.'

'I'll bet.'

'The High Twelve is fracturing, Drakan. They could be coherent, at least, when they knew that Udo could pander to their interests, but now there is *that*.' Veritus pointed skyward. He didn't put a name to it, as though it was a dae-mon that could be summoned by stating it. 'The paralysis, the disbelief – it was no different when Horus brought the armies of Chaos to Terra. No one, perhaps not even the Emperor Himself, believed that it could happen, even after it had already begun. Terra survived the Siege that followed only because Rogal Dorn united a factionalised military, and wielded them with one will.'

'You're talking about a primarch.'

'I am talking about strong leadership. The High Lords would back it if they saw it.'

Vangorich shook his head sadly. Another age, another class of man. One could not simply replace a demigod. There wasn't one man amongst the Imperium's countless trillions who could even come close.

But who said it had to be a man? What if it could be some-thing more?

'We can speak more at the Senatorum tomorrow,' said Veritus tiredly, angling his body pointedly to open a path to the door. 'I trust that you can find your own way out.'

'I did find my way in,' said Vangorich, surfacing from his thoughts and making to leave. He paused inside the door-way and turned back.

'Where is Wienand?'

'You betray your care, Drakan.'

'Or reinforce your preconceptions.'

A genuine smile stretched at Veritus' face. 'She works towards the common end, as the Emperor's Inquisition always will.'

'And your... guest?'

The suite was cloaked with a counter-surveillance manifold, both technological and arcane, and was covered by a psychically generated blanket of silence. But even with only Veritus in the room and Krule outside who could possibly overhear, it felt unwise to mention their xenos captive by name. It was like Veritus and the ork moon. Naming the thing gave it a life beyond one's control.

'Helpful,' said Veritus, simply.

Vangorich let it go. He had more pressing matters on his mind.

Beast Krule was waiting in the foyer, sitting on the edge of a woven aluminium chair. He unfolded himself as Vangorich walked towards him.

'Problems?'

Vangorich shook his head. 'Does Esad Wire still have his uniform?'

'He's been off duty for a long time. Even in KVF Sub Twelve that kind of absence without leave gets noticed.'

'You won't be going back to Tashkent. I want you to find the Provost-Marshal.'

'I can do that, sir. What made you decide on him?'

'Nothing so terminal. I need you to deliver him a message. Tell him he has my guarantee that he'll want to be at the Senatorum tomorrow.'

TEN

First Captain Zerberyn came round to the squeal of plasma tools and the smell of sparks. The emergency lighting was low and sporadic, the shadows long. Wired multilaser cradles hung from their rails, limp and unpowered, and flecked with white specks of flame-retardant spray. The rough shape of Marcarian's head passed between Zerberyn and *Dantalion*'s ceiling. The light nicked the shipmaster's steel frame.

'We made it,' Zerberyn croaked.

His throat was bruised. Talking felt like trying to swallow a rank pin.

He grunted and rolled his head, his eye at floor level, and looked along the deck plates to one of the command turrets. Sparks sputtered from torn electrics. A team of serfs in full-body protective gear and rebreather kit attacked a fallen bulkhead with a plasma torch. Charged filaments of waste plasma crackled and sprayed. The stuttering light silhouetted a robed figure casting cleansing oils around the cut site, reciting a psalm for the ship's forgiveness and

fast healing. A giant amongst those lesser mortals in his unmarked battleplate, Veteran-Sergeant Columba was bent into the heart of the plasma spray, pulling away chunks of debris in his gauntleted hands and hurling them over the edge to clang in the cogitation pit below.

'Vox,' Zerberyn recognised. 'The last thing I remember... I was at Operations. Your crew allowed the dorsal void bank to overload.'

'An inevitable consequence of going into battle with a numerical, strategic, and technological disadvantage, lord captain,' slurred Marcarian, stumping clumsily into his field of view. 'An emitter overload when we translated out threw you down the walkway and struck your head on the rail. You've been out for just over an hour.' He shrugged apologetically, or tried to. 'I'm not sure exactly how long. The chronos are out.'

With a groan, Zerberyn made to pull in his elbows and draw himself up.

Nothing moved.

In consternation more than concern, he jerked on his arms, then his legs, but neither moved a millimetre. He could feel them, a pins-and-needles tingle across his various points of contact with the ground, but he couldn't command a single muscle to twitch. It was as though the servo-muscular connections to his armour had been severed. Without power assistance and nervous control, half a tonne of bonded ceramite was little more than an ornate null-sensoria tank, the kind used to prepare neophytes for the experience of mucranoid hibernation.

Indignity piled upon indignity.

'I cannot move.'

Marcarian gestured across his body with an open palm. Zerberyn rolled his head the other way, and met the leering half-skull of Mendel Reoch.

The Space Marine's armour was bone-white and bore the modified double-helix of the Apothecarium on the shoulder pad. All well within the diktats laid down in the *Codex Astartes*, and Zerberyn therefore felt obligated to approve, but, as with the Chaplaincy black, it seemed inimical to the Exemplar spirit. An alternative variable was that Zerberyn simply did not like Reoch. And he *did* dislike his Second Company brother, with a self-sustaining passion. Binoptics glowered dully from the eye-pits of the organic upper half of the Apothecary's face, the lower part constructed by the ugly fusion of an iron grille to the son of Dorn's once-noble cheekbones. The reconstructive work was so extensive, so obtrusive that given the Apothecary's long service and skill its unsightliness could only have been intentional, as if Reoch had deliberately cut back his face to bare cold metal, and a darkness he no longer wanted to conceal.

'You will heal. Your paralysis is induced and temporary.' His voice was a grizzle of vox-corruption. His optics glimmered with every intonation. 'I have noted an alarming tendency amongst our Chapter brothers to not lie still when commanded to do so.'

Zerberyn held Reoch's unblinking, back-lit stare.

'Flush it out of me. Now.'

Reoch sighed. 'I blame Oriax Dantalion. He persuaded the primarch-progenitor to adopt the *Codex Astartes* and now every Exemplar believes himself a martyr to his own special wisdom.'

DAVID GUYMER

'Except for you of course, brother.'

'I am an Apothecary,' said Reoch. The diamantine drill-bit of his narthecium gauntlet revved and reversed. A spring-loaded injector attachment clicked out of the reductor, cycled through various combinations of syringes and needles until a hyperfine carbon tip slotted into a slender glass vial, locked, then extended forwards. The plunger drew back into the apparatus, slowly filling the syringe with a milky fluid as the Apothecary leaned in. 'I always know best.'

Zerberyn clenched his jaw and tilted his head to expose the vulnerable fibre bundles and cabling hidden beneath the gorget ring. He felt a sharp pain as the hypodermic squeezed between the vertebrae at the top of his spine, and then a rush of cold. He gave an involuntary gasp, then shuddered as the sensation passed down his spinal cord and dispersed into his peripheral nervous system. He wriggled his fingers and this time they moved, gauntlet servos whirring as armoured digits rolled clumsily in and out, up and down. On impulse, he shifted his hand to fumble over his weapons belt.

His fingers closed around the grip of his bolt pistol and squeezed. Fingers, wrist, shoulders: the sensation of being bundled up in a skin-tight carapace of thick wool began to recede. An Umbra-pattern bolt pistol's uncompromising menace left no place in its proximity for that kind of uncertainty.

He sat up slowly.

A tangle of twisted and torn walkways crisscrossed the command deck, smoke and dust rising from the cogitation pits with each slow grinding *whup* of fans. The strategium display was static, the encircling image-boosters and visual feeds hissing noise. The main viewer crackled with electromagnetic distortions, flickering with augur traces and warp energy residuals that stained the eye with afterghosts. Everywhere the frail bodies of crew serfs lay under blood-lashed metal.

Anger, real anger deep in his transhuman belly, filled him with excoriating fire.

A Chapter-strength deployment, the might of the Fists Exemplar fleet, had been brushed aside. Ship to ship, man to man, the Adeptus Astartes would always triumph, but the weapons and technologies that the Beast could call on were just too powerful. *Dantalion* transported the bulk of the First Company, a few squads of the Second, Seventh and Tenth. What had happened to the rest of the fleet? *Bulwark*, *Faceless Warrior*? *Alcazar Remembered*? Could the Fists Exemplar have been reduced to little more than the First Company and a handful of squads from three others?

There had been no other option. Any other commander of the Fists Exemplar would have taken the same decision as him.

'How did this happen?'

'We were not as worthy as we considered ourselves to be,' answered Reoch, clenching the reductor back into his narthecium as he turned and walked away.

Marcarian stepped back to allow Zerberyn to stand up, the Space Marine's genetic gifts just about compensating for the dizziness and slight lack of motor control that lingered in his system courtesy of Mendel Reoch. The bruising round his neck restricted his range of motion, but breathing at least came easier now that he was upright.

'What is our status?'

'The orks took out the system. The whole damned system. We were lucky, if you'd call it luck. We were already heading out, and were able to make an emergency translation before we suffered too much heavy damage.' A ruptured power conduit running through the ceiling sprayed the walkway with sparks and made the shipmaster flinch. 'The rest we suffered during,' he shouted, as the hiss of sparks died down. 'I saw the *Interdictor* make it out ahead of us. I also saw *Grey Ranger* crushed like she was nothing.' He was silent a moment. 'My first ship.'

'Did any other ships manage to escape?'

'No sign yet, but it's only been ten minutes or so since we emerged. Systems are still coming back online and we're still assessing the damage. And...'

He gestured to the wreck of the vox-turret.

'Suggestions?'

The Fists Exemplar hierarchy was no different to that of any other Codex-compliant Chapter, but the lines were enforced with a stringency seldom seen elsewhere. They were notoriously free and independent thinkers in their founder's mould: not the barbaric affectation of the Wolves of Fenris, nor the solitary temperament of the hunters of Mundus Planus, but a mentality born of absolute conviction their personal infallibility. It was, when properly managed, their greatest strength.

'The Codex would suggest we resume our original heading,' said Marcarian. 'If anyone made it out of Vandis then they could be anywhere in the subsector. Rejoining the Last Wall at Phall would be their most logical destination.'

'I doubt the ship would survive such a journey,' Zerberyn grunted as he stood. 'Walk with me to Vox.'

There was not a lot to see. Zerberyn picked up a headset from a console. Foam covered it. The loop of wire by which it was plugged into the terminal pulled taut as he drew it to his face, a child's toy in his massive gauntlet.

'Where is the woman that was stationed here?'

Marcarian nodded to the work crew. Their plasma torch was making rasping, shallow cuts into the bulkhead that had sliced the section in half. And Marcarian's vox-liaison too, by the looks of it. The hiss and whine of spent plasma was strangely reminiscent of the white noise leaching from the transceiver set, as if there was some cosmic confluence of which Zerberyn, for all his gifts, could never be anything but unaware.

'A shame,' he said, and meant it. She had been competent.

Marcarian toed aside the twisted aluminium frame of a console chair, taking the ivory sliders and brass dials and deftly recalibrating the board. Zerberyn pushed the left headset earpiece up against his corresponding ear and listened.

White noise whispered from the set. Static. Which was a misnomer in many ways. It implied a steady state, something unchanging, but the sound crying through *Dantalion*'s receiver arrays was anything but steady. It crested and fell, hissed and crackled, and precipitously dropped or rose in pitch. It was cosmic background noise, stellar radiation, energy bleed from unshielded power sources – which, on the command deck just then, must have numbered anywhere in the high thousands. It was almost like voices, whispers at the very edge of straining.

'Stop!'

A horrible sensation chased down Zerberyn's spine, similar to the feeling of the counteractant that the Apothecary had injected into him but a hundredfold worse for having no discernable material source. As if a soul could feel rotten. As if static had the taste of copper and smoke. He tightened his grip on the physical surety of the headset and turned to Marcarian.

'Dial it back.'

The shipmaster did so. The noise dropped away, to be replaced by a sound in his head like knives on the wind. It *was* a voice.

+*Dantalion... Dantalion*, respond.+

'The system is fried,' Marcarian was saying, a vox-wraith in his other ear. 'It's the receiver. It can't distinguish signal from noise.'

'Do not touch the controls,' Zerberyn snapped. He felt sick. Not physically of course – his gifts prevented that – but he felt spiritually spoiled. He twisted around the headset's microphone bulb and spoke into it. 'Is that you, Epistolary? Is this *Guilliman*?'

A sound like laughter prickled the static.

+My name is Kalkator, Warsmith of the Fourth Legion, in command of the cruiser *Palimodes*.+

Zerberyn froze. He wanted nothing more than to tear the headset from his face, but it was as though the absolute cold of the void had soaked into *Dantalion*'s antennae, run through her wires, and iced the muffler to Zerberyn's ear.

'I do not speak with traitors,' he hissed.

+Then just listen. You are in danger here. Your jump has not taken you far from the ruins of Vandis. Your vessels

Paragon and *Intrepid* are in the Corus System. *Paladin of Rubicae* is in Randeil and *Vindicator* in Quaillor. *Guilliman* and *Excelsior* are in the Ooran System. None more than an hour from an ork fleet. And trust me, *Dantalion*, they are coming.+

'Trust you...?'

Marcarian was looking up at him, uncomprehending. Some horror in his eyes made the bruised skin at the back of Zerberyn's neck creep. He spoke again into the pickup.

'How do you know the coordinates of our ships? How are you reaching us?'

+Favours given, favours owed. Do you really want those kinds of answers, Exemplar?+

'What of the rest of the fleet?' he said after an uncomfortably extended pause. 'What of *Alcazar Remembered*? What of the *Interdictor*?'

+You are the last to emerge and I had almost given up on the possibility of any more of your ships making it from the warp intact. My ship made it to the Mandeville point and was primed for translation when Vandis was destroyed. The empyrean buffered her systems against the star's death throes.+

'An escape paid for in the blood of my brothers. No depth of space could obscure from me the warmth you show your allies, Iron Warrior.'

The voice dropped into the seethe of static. Zerberyn could hear the crackle of emotion.

+There was a time when Magneric and I were thought closer than brothers. Our bond was stronger than I expect you to understand, forged by the glories of an age you

cannot conceive. I found his faith contemptible, his obses-
sion with me pitiable. Magneric would be even less fulsome
in his remembrance of me were our fates reversed, but I will
remember him as a brother. Do you think your Imperium
the sole proprietor of a finite store of grief? We are not so
different, you and I.+

'How so?'

+Did pragmatism not lead you to abandon your own
Chapter Master?+

'We did not see the *Alcazar Remembered* destroyed.'

+I did not see the Emperor slay Horus, but I know that
it was so.+

Zerberyn snarled. 'Do not ever forget it.'

+For one who chooses not to speak, you are as lyrical as
any scion of Sanguinius. I asked you to listen, now listen.
There is a system less than three hours from you – Prax. It
was a garrison world of the Iron Warriors at the height of the
Great Crusade and if there is a single world within ten light
years that the orks' advance into Segmentum Solar has not
already destroyed, then it will be that upon which sit Perturabo's walls. If we can muster our assets over Prax, then
we might all have a chance of going our separate ways.+

This time, Zerberyn managed to pull the headset off.

His chest felt tight, but hollow, as if his armour plate was
wrapped like a mummy's bindings around an over-inflated
skin. He smothered the headset pickup in his gauntlet, and
turned to Marcarian.

The cruiser *Paladin of Rubicae* transported the Fifth and
the Ninth, while the mighty *Guilliman* held the bulk of
the Second as well as elements of the Third, Fourth, Tenth

and most of what *Dantalion* didn't carry of the First. Three, maybe three hundred and fifty brothers. Add the firepower of the aegis frigates, *Paragon, Intrepid* and *Vindicator*, and the support frigate *Excelsior*, and it was clear that one run-down traitor cruiser presented little by way of a tangible material threat.

And of the other kind, that less physical peril?

He licked dry lips, mentally crunching variables he had never before now had cause to quantify or weigh relative to others. He attacked his scheme of action from every angle, however improbable, assessing with force the firmness of every assumption on which it was founded until what remained was a bastion of solid calculation and impregnable logic.

He was an Exemplar.

Infallible.

He returned the headset to his ear and uncovered the pickup.

'Send me the coordinates.'

ELEVEN

Prax – approach

Dantalion slid out of warp space into the dust-banded outer reaches of the Prax System like a jammed magazine ejected from an overheating boltgun. Proximity alert tocsins added a deep basso two-tone to the symphonic chorus of alarms. The auspex was still powering up, but proximity detection was a passive system, its workings founded upon the innate sense that certain metals possessed for metal. At the same time, triggered automatically by the completion of the translation cycle, the command deck's blast shutters were rolling back.

Crew-serfs and Space Marines looked up from rebooting consoles and covered their eyes. The starlight was hard and bright, the guide lights of a monster voidship burning like a meteor shower off the bow. The garish yellow vessel was several times more massive than *Dantalion* and of eccentric design. Modules stuck out from a long central body, like landing booms on a seaplane but coming out at all angles and in various shapes and sizes. The slender main body widened at the neck to give a bulbous prow and, towards the stern, grew by stepwise tiers towards a garishly hazard-striped housing for the fierce orange cones of the drive exhaust. Sitting atop the drive housing, adding half again to the height of the stern, was a crescent moon, bent and crooked into a vile facsimile of a grinning orkoid face.

'Thrusters!' called Shipmaster Marcarian. 'Hard port. Decompress starboard launch bays and fire macro-batteries. All the push we have.'

The ork ship pulled away slowly, port thrusters burning hard to win some traction over the vacuum. A lumpen module, riveted plates hatched yellow and black, swung out towards *Dantalion*'s starboard-side viewing ports, close enough for Zerberyn to see the alien pictographs scrawled onto its side. Then, the ship winked out, something darker than space rushing out to envelop it. Torpedoes and other mass-weapons winnowed through the hole left in real space.

'Another ship inbound,' called the seated hardline operator reporting from auspectoria. 'Throne, they're everywhere. Two thousand kilometres in-system. And another in convoy, the exact same spacing again.'

Zerberyn snarled. 'As if surrendering ourselves to the Imperial Fists is not betrayal enough, we must contend with Iron Warriors treachery. Charge weapons and prepare to fire.'

'Wait,' said Marcarian, looking out of a port-side viewport at the next incoming ship. 'No torpedo apertures, no flight decks, no weapon batteries that I can see except a handful of flak turrets, no energy spike on our scans to indicate they're powering them up. I think that ship is unarmed.'

'When did you ever see an unarmed ork ship?'

'My point exactly. Helm, move us out of the path of the traffic. Five hundred kilometres to port. Auspectoria, commence scans for our brothers.'

'Ayes' acknowledged his instructions. *Dantalion* swung deeper into her portside yaw. The ork ships held true to their course.

'Arrogant xenos,' Zerberyn muttered, watching the unaugmented view through a viewport. The image booster screens around Strategium continued to snow. 'They lack even the good sense to alter course to avoid our weapons.'

'We are one ship, lord captain, and a damaged one at that. I would posit that they don't consider us a threat.'

'Then I posit that we purge them of that unwise presumption.'

'Lords.' Auspectoria again, the operative already swivelling his chair back around to point to the sensorium feed being relayed in précis to his monitor. Zerberyn and Marcarian joined him. The Space Marine towered above the two serfs, looking over the sloping bank of hardline wires into the din and confusion of the recovery work still ongoing around them. 'Receivers are picking up a lot of vox-chatter. Numerical sequences, auto-broadcasts. Well over ten thousand ships, most of them concentrated here.' He tapped the screen with his fingernail. 'The third planet.'

'Prax,' said Zerberyn.

It was a guess: the last avenue of retreat for reactionaries and for mortals impelled to wage total war on inscrutable xenos-breeds and demi-gods. But it was an educated one.

'Prax,' the operator duly confirmed. 'Archives list it as an agri-world and subsector governance hub. Limited orbital and dry-dock facilities, but nothing to permit shipping on this scale. Whatever the orks are using to coordinate so many vessels, they brought it in from elsewhere or built it themselves.'

'Look at the disposition of these ships,' said Marcarian, leaning over the serf's shoulder to float his fingertip over the display. He turned to Zerberyn, ear-stud catching the green of the screen, and grinned. 'Did your duty ever take you along the Eukrist Corridor, galactic east through the Flux with a layover at Angels' Wake Munitorum star port?'

'Humour me, shipmaster.'

Marcarian's nerveless lips hung a smile. 'It looked like this.'

'A supply hub? An ork Administratum?'

'Except orks don't think that way,' Marcarian continued. 'They exploit the worlds they come to and then move on. Like at Ardamantua.'

'They are building,' said Zerberyn. A smile, slow and angry, began to spread and he turned it on Marcarian. 'He must be close. The Beast. If not here, then somewhere near.'

Marcarian stumped again to the viewport and looked out. 'I wonder what that symbol means. That crescent moon shape on their ships. Some kind of merchant class, do you think?'

A handset in the partially restored vox-turret blinked and chimed. The new duty liaison took the missive standing up and turned to face Zerberyn.

'Incoming transmission from *Palimodes*, and from *Guilliman*. Coming through the hololith grid.'

Zerberyn was surprised to feel disappointed. In turbulent

times, it was reassuring to know that the galaxy continued to rotate and the traitors would forever be traitors.

'Patch them through,' Marcarian ordered, and turned to face the display.

Power built up within the arcane suspension of coils and valves with a succession of etheric metal bangs, as though the device's spirit railed against its reactivation so soon after translation. Tech-serfs stroked power distribution sliders and capacitance dials in a bid to soothe its anguish, and coaxed the weary machine to compliance. Two faces took shape within the loop projector. The face to the left of the static divider, cowled within a high grey hood, was familiar, even if the penetrating eyes looked pained and the ancient face drawn. Epistolary Honorius of *Guilliman* greeted Zerberyn's image with a nod.

That other face, however...

Unconsciously Zerberyn drew himself to his full, impressive height, resolved to meet the image's gaze like a Space Marine.

The stranger was dust pale and cadaverously thin, as though the withdrawal of the Emperor's love had left him withered and bitter. His hollow cheeks made his sharp jawline cruel, and accentuated his high brow to something arch and not quite fully human. His eyes glinted like nails under the unforgiving light of his ship's hololith projector.

'It is good to talk face to face at last,' said Kalkator.

Zerberyn had expected the traitor's voice to match the forsaken character of his appearance, but it was surprisingly rich and powerful. It was a voice Zerberyn could well imagine sharing a field with the primarchs.

An unworthy flutter of jealousy – no, worse – of *curiosity*, disturbed the calm beating of his hearts.

'Indeed, you are as pleasing a sight as the great garrison world of your forsaken brothers.'

'It has been a long time devoid of our care,' Kalkator replied. 'Had this world still been defended by my brothers, then the situation would have been different.'

'Had these worlds still been loyally defended by Iron Warriors,' said Epistolary Honorius, eyes far away and long ago, 'then many things would be different.'

'It will have to serve, regardless,' said Kalkator, turning back to Zerberyn. 'Your ship will not survive another transit through the warp. Not without repairs. And mine will not survive without yours.'

'We are sending a navigation packet,' Honorius continued, gesturing to something or someone off-capture.

Marcarian limped to the nearest functioning terminal and activated it, telemetrics and data-icons turning his pale face green. 'The eighth planet. An Ouranos-class ice giant with a ring system in a near-perpendicular orbit. The coordinates are for a geostationary position above the northern magnetic pole, inside the rings.' He smiled, impressed. 'I'm afraid the diffraction index of the magnetosphere and the rings is too much for our auspex.'

'The orks' no less,' said Kalkator. 'If their technical prowess extends beyond firepower and propulsion then they have yet to show it here.'

Looking across the image of the Traitor Space Marine, Zerberyn addressed the other figure. 'What is your condition, Epistolary?'

'If you ask after me personally, then I must confess I have been better. The ork psyker aboard that carrier was uncommonly powerful. His effect on me was... intense. But I will recover. With Thane's foresight *Guilliman* and *Excelsior* exited the battle at Vandis with minimal damage, but *Paragon*, *Courageous* and *Implicit* will require extensive repair. Of *Paladin of Rubicae* and *Vindicator* there remains no sign and no word. We had almost given up hope on you also, First Captain. We have been waiting for several hours.'

Marcarian gestured for and promptly received a data-slate, then tapped at it before turning to Zerberyn. 'Real time confirmed and verified: translation plus twenty-two hours and eleven minutes.' He handed the slate back to the serf. 'See that *Dantalion*'s timepieces are updated.'

Zerberyn let out a rough breath.

If the orks' teleportation capability ameliorated just some of the uncertainties of warp transit then it would be a decisive technological edge, far more so than the gravitational weaponry they had deployed at Vandis. The vagaries of the warp were the rate-limiting factor in any galaxy-scale endeavour. Fleets heading towards the same point from equidistant systems could never be relied upon to arrive even within days of one another. An astropathic message cast into the immaterium from Terra could make it to Alpha Centauri in a week or in a month, and could as easily reach distant Occludus first. It turned keeping track of thousands of active fleet and military elements and an evolving tactical situation played out over segmenta into a logistical nightmare: a challenge that would tax even the mind of a primarch.

'If we are to remain here, then we must take advantage of the opportunity this presents us,' said Zerberyn. 'Orks do not settle, orks do not trade, and yet here they are. We must find out what they are up to here, and in such numbers. The orks appear content to ignore us for now.'

'A desirable state of affairs given our current condition,' Kalkator cut in.

'Is there anything you can discern here, Epistolary?' asked Zerberyn through gritted teeth.

'The Emperor has granted me no further insight since our departure from Terra, but I have had little opportunity to meditate on the matter these last few days.' Honorius sank back into what looked like a command throne and closed his eyes. 'You have rank, First Captain. I am minded to agree with the warsmith, but I will support any decision you make.'

'It is made, Epistolary.'

Kalkator emitted a long-suffering sigh. 'On your own head be it.'

'I do not ask for your approval.'

'Good. Because I withhold it, *little cousin*. But Prax is our world, and if you insist on this course then I too must insist on accompanying you to the surface. Our chances of survival will not be aided by the deaths of you and your warriors.'

Zerberyn glowered. And why not? The greatest impossibility conceivable in his existence, as the decree of Roboute Guilliman and the legacy of Oriax Dantalion had always defined it, had already been borne out with the reformation of the VII Legion. Where was the line now? One more broken rule? Two? Was there still a line?

'One squad each.'

'Agreed.'

Kalkator's pallid features drew into a smile. Zerberyn met the warsmith's gaze, as cold and grey without as his true armour within.

TWELVE

Terra – the Imperial Palace

Drakan Vangorich knelt at the shrine to light a candle. There were more to choose between than would ordinarily be the case. The handful already lit burned low, wicks struggling to hold their heads above ever deepening pools of molten wax.

The chapel ordinary was an austere stone cell lacking even a window to distract one's mind from communion with the God-Emperor. It was generally used by Palace servants and householders for their daily observances, but Vangorich found its asceticism useful. It made him look humble, civilised and discreet. He was, in fact, all of those things, but no one ever lit a candle or left a coin in a collection bowl to affirm their own virtues to themselves. It was an elaborate masquerade, a game in which no one played the part that their costumes dictated, a performance each and every day of his life so that the ever-circling Palace spies might see the Vangorich that Vangorich wished their masters to see. In so doing, he had allowed himself to become almost as hollow as the part he played.

Some habits were hard to break. Even now, with a twenty-four hour curfew of the entire Inner Palace in preparation for the day's Senatorum business, he maintained the charade of piety.

Vangorich blew out the lighting taper and dropped the smouldering tip into a jar of sand.

Despite his reputation, he was not a creature of solitude. Any number of unfortunate incidents could befall an individual when he was alone. He was in a position to know. Krule was, of course, no more than thirty seconds away, and he himself was by no means defenceless. A man did not rise to become Grand Master of the Officio Assassinorum without possessing skills, but he also knew how far those skills could serve him. This was not a galaxy that rewarded the hubris of men.

Suddenly, he felt the unexpected and rather uncomfortable need to pray. He was a faithful man, of a kind, observant through rote if not from a true spirituality. He appeared to pray because it served him to be seen to pray.

As he generally made these shows of devotion prior to Senatorum meetings – the better to make oneself receptive to the will and wisdom of the God-Emperor – his thoughts had often revolved around upcoming business. Intelligence briefings on unredacted leaks of pre-agenda packets, comprehensively war-gamed conversational cues to feed the High Twelve. Often, but not always. The Imperium was vast, the Officio ever-busy. There had always been something with which to occupy his mind during a peaceful spell.

And yet for all the occasions that he had knelt here in this chapel and closed his eyes for the spies and vid-capture drones, he had never gone so far as to actually pray. It had never seemed necessary to carry the deception that far. He closed his eyes again.

This seemed to be the way most people went about it.

After a minute or two of stray thoughts, he became aware of the entry of another through the doorless stone arch that led into the chapel from the base of Daylight Wall.

His powers of observation were attuned rather than enhanced, a product of training, conditioning and – over the course of his career – natural selection. On this occasion however, no special talent was required. It was difficult to tread softly when one was half again the height of a normal man and encased like a warrior-knight of ancient Terra in plasteel and ceramite.

'There is a curfew in force in this area, citizen,' said Koorland, his voice, even unaugmented by helm or speaker, resonant and compelling.

Vangorich turned. He remained on his knees.

The Imperial Fist was magnificent in his armour. He was strength and grace, the expression on his face that which a small child might perceive upon a domineering but ultimately protective father. Through superhuman *breadth* alone he projected an aura of invincibility. Vangorich knew this to be false, but even so he felt it, and could understand why so many had faith in the power of the Adeptus Astartes to be the wall between humanity and its enemies. Koorland was a sight to stir the soul, to excite the subliminal with imagery of angels and immortals and god-kings armoured in gold.

'As a matter of fact I was just thinking about that,' said

Vangorich. 'It's reassuring that the Senatorum retains some ability to function when their best interests are served, wouldn't you agree?'

'My apologies, Grand Master,' said Koorland, recognition easing the sternness from his features. 'This is a simple shrine. Had I realised that you prayed here I would have made allowances.'

'I'm surprised you recognised me,' Vangorich smiled. 'There are people I see every day who wouldn't remember my face. It's something I'm rather proud of.'

'My apologies again,' Koorland returned, humourless. 'I do not forget a face.'

'Or anything else, I suspect. I have a gift for recollection myself, though nothing like yours. You surpass me in almost every way conceivable, don't you? As you were designed to surpass us all.'

'I fight and serve, that is all. But,' he crossed his arms, dazzling by candlelight, 'you did not seek me out to deliver a compliment. And you *did* seek me out, Grand Master.'

Vangorich conceded a shrug, and then stood.

'I find myself struggling with what to call you. Plain "Koorland" doesn't quite do your position justice. Chapter Master no longer seems entirely appropriate either.'

'You could call me Slaughter.'

Vangorich felt that he was expected to smile, and did. The Imperial Fist did not.

'A pleasure speaking with you, Grand Master,' said Koorland, turning away.

'The defence of Terra permits no rest, does it?' Vangorich called after the Space Marine's broad shoulders. 'Your diligence in preparing the Palace's defences has been inspirational. Given the circumstances.'

'I hold,' said Koorland, face half turned over the black fist that emblazoned his left pauldron. 'That is my duty. The circumstances are never irrelevant, but they will never change that fact.'

'When I walk the Palace grounds I see Space Marines on the walls again. I realise that they can never replace the Imperial Fists, and yet Daylight, the others, the symbol they now wear...'

Koorland's gaze dropped almost imperceptibly, brushing the curve of his pauldron plate – the black fist on its white field.

This time Vangorich's smile was his own and quite genuine. Guile and discretion were the principal tools of his Officio, but there always came the time when an operative had to step out of the shadows and show the knife. Metaphorically, of course. But the good ones, the really good ones, could time their move so perfectly, manoeuvre their weapon so expertly, that they never wound up with blood on their hands.

'You have been an inspiration even to them, lord. And the regular forces even more so. The Lucifer Blacks have worn, well, black, since before the Unification Wars, but I believe I have seen some yellow starting to appear these past weeks. They worship you, and I'm not speaking figuratively – you are as close to the God-Emperor as any of them will ever come.'

Koorland turned back. 'I do not serve for accolades.'

'Higher words of praise were never spoken within these

walls, trust me. But from whom do you think those soldiers would rather take their orders? Some distant lord who hasn't set foot beyond the Inner Palace since greasing his way out of the Navy, or one of the true defenders of humanity?'

'I fight, I serve and I hold. That is all.'

Vangorich tilted his head back and looked pointedly up. A hairline fracture ran across the chapel's ceiling, a millimetre incontinuity where the latest round of tremors had moved the north wall marginally westward relative to the south. This was a minor shrine, frequented by nobody of importance but the Grand Master of a shadowy Officio that few higher authorities much cared for. The repair detail was mired in the bureaucracy of the Administratum.

'We need more from you. If the orks tire of our dithering tomorrow and launch their assault, what will happen? Can you hold Terra without the full backing of the Astra Militarum? Let's say that you can, that you do, and that we are all still here to conduct the hunt for the Beast that you have been calling for. Do you really want to do it fighting the Navy, the Astropathica, and the Administratum every step of the way?'

Koorland said nothing. It was an opening, and Vangorich took it.

'You do wish to confront the Beast?'

'A firm defence is central to the avoidance of defeat, but a strategy of containment will never win a war. The Siege was the greatest defensive action in history, but it was the Emperor's defeat of Horus that finally ended the Heresy.'

'Politics is very much like war,' Vangorich agreed softly.

'Sometimes the only solution is to strike for the figure at the top.'

'I serve the Imperium loyally,' Koorland returned, shocked, angry.

Sometimes a failing organ needed to be shocked, Vangorich thought.

'Have you paused recently to ask yourself what the Imperium really needs?'

The Imperial Fist fell silent, his eyes running deep.

Vangorich offered a slight bow and left the transhuman to his thoughts. He was not nearly important enough that the Senatorum would wait on his arrival, and Koorland had a lot to think about.

THIRTEEN

Prax

The matt-grey Thunderhawk gunship *Penitence* descended hard on the planet's night side, ventral thrusters blasting up a tsunami of dust as the assault craft levelled out and dropped its troop doors. Dust billowed through the open hatch, whipping through handgrips and cargo netting and smothering the armoured forms of Veteran Squad Anatoq. With the enhanced senses of smell and taste granted by his neuroglottis, Zerberyn sifted the storm of particulates. Small stones. Dead soil. Bone chips. Blood. It chopped up the twelve helmet beams and the weak pastel glow of wall-mounted panels, banging and rattling inside the troop compartment.

'Quickly in and quickly out,' voxed Veteran-Sergeant Columba over the squad channel, one hand wrapped around a ceiling handgrip.

The sergeant was an iron-faced ascetic with ice water in his veins and heart of leaden grey. A narrow view of the Fists Exemplar creed of humility had led him to turn down

the captaincy of the First more than once, and he had pub-
lically rebuked Koorland over the offer of a position in the
reformed shield corps of Terra. Zerberyn liked him.

The narrow beam of his own helm light cut half a metre
into the swirl, catching the whipped-up grit as if by surprise, stripping it from uniform night-black to white and
grey and bloody brown. A crowd of gold runes representative of his squad slid around the periphery of his internal
faceplate display, the gunship's shaking, under the force of
its own engines, unsettling the runes' positions. The boarding ramp railroaded out into the dark. He could see neither
the ground nor the end of the ramp.

'We are Exemplars,' he said into his helm vox. 'No wall
stands against us. No wall can stand beside us.'

'You all know your objectives,' Columba concluded.

Zerberyn led them into the vertical jetwash, running, a
servo-powered leap plunging him into a rippling funnel of
dust. For a moment a combination of his battleplate's powered systems and the updraught of disturbed earth made
him fly. Then he fell, five metres, half a tonne of ceramite
slamming two-footed into dry earth. Suspensor grids dispersed the impact force throughout his armour, plates
shifting, crunching to a crouch, then with a counter-whine
of servos he came up, disengaged his pistol's mag-holster
and whipped the weapon up.

He could not see a thing. Dust devils gyrated between the
ground and the gunship's thundering exhausts, sieving the
landing lights from above. Blinking runes in his helm display and the vibrations picked up by his boot sensors told
of veteran-brothers thumping into the ground around him.

They fanned out from the drop zone, murky giants with boltguns raised and aimed.

Veteran-Brother Donbuss was triple-checking the belt feed to his heavy bolter and covering the advance from relative high ground. Antille dropped to one knee, hand to where his ear was underneath his helmet, the long antennae of a shoulder-mounted vox-booster whipping above him. Each Space Marine's battleplate was independently vox-capable, but the volume of near-orbit communications noise and the signal diffraction of their own fleet's place in hiding necessitated the booster should they need to raise their brothers around the eighth planet. Apothecary Reoch stood nearby holding his narthecium at arm's length, sampling the wind for toxin traces or pathogens. It was almost impossible to kill a Space Marine by such means, but a reasonable excess of caution won more wars than abandon ever had. Veteran-Brother Karva was the twelfth and last down, pivoting on the spot as a promethium tank dropped through the darkness and catching it in the crook of his arms.

Zerberyn voxed up to the Thunderhawk that his squad was deployed, received two brittle clicks through his microbead in response, and then felt a slam of downwash.

With a tremendous roar of thrust, the gunship rose, re-angling its engines for horizontal flight, and pulled away. The dust storm began to settle, stones and larger debris falling to leave dried organic matter zipping about. It cleared the air enough for Zerberyn to see *Penitence* turning for a fly-past of the planet's principal city, Princus Praxa, and its Crusade fortress approximately two hundred kilometres east across the daylight meridian.

A second gunship circled in low. Its metallic bodywork was embellished with unorthodox modifications: battle honours, ablative hull plating and variant weapon loadouts – not all of it was of obvious human make. The star-backed iron skull of the Iron Warriors stared grimly from its tailfin and nose section. Keeping low, it banked left and began to steadily climb, mapping the terrain with a pair of sweeping spotlights and searching for an appropriate drop-zone of its own.

Zerberyn processed his surroundings without thinking about it.

Left, a diagonal line of wind power converters, bi-blades, chomping sombrely through the dark. A greasy metal water tank, empty, riddled with holes, fenced off with wire that had been cut and trampled. Brother Tarsus advanced, boltgun sweeping the row of quietly whumping turbines.

Right, looming rockcrete-walled slurry pits, surrounded by dirty metal outbuildings. A petrochem generator. A silage tank, round-walled and massive. One of the sheds was a machine store. It was open, an upswinging outer door half-covering a weather-beaten wheeled truck. The vehicle was a rusted contraption of belts, pulleys, and funnels, with an articulated pallet lifter at the front end painted to look like an orkish mouth. It had a canvas top and a blood-splattered rear fender. Its tyres were flat. Brothers Galen and Borhune took firing positions, Karva moving up to cover the units with his heavy flamer. Behind, nothing, according to the Thunderhawk's deep augur scans – just over-exploited pastureland and dust.

Ahead, the objective.

His enhanced low-light vision described the structure in sharp detail. It was a massive, industrialised agricultural unit, with dust-tanned steel walls and barred windows. A large, rectangular glyph of a twisting serpent had been graffitied over the upper storey windows. It was an ork structure, but it was only as Zerberyn closed and metrics gathered in his helm display that he realised that every feature was about twenty-five per cent too large for human standard. The dirt drive leading up to the main door was churned with tyre tracks and strewn with bone meal, dung and what looked like scraps of clothing.

He loped forwards at an easy run. Brothers Hardran and Nalis followed up behind, flanking and covering the upper storeys and secondary entrances with their bolters. Tosque and Columba kept pace, the former maintaining his aim on the door with a bulky combi-plasma.

The unit frequency crackled in Zerberyn's ear.

'Galen. No contacts.'

'Tarsus. Same here, brother-captain.'

'Reoch,' voxed the Apothecary, voice double-distorted and animal. 'I am reading high soil concentrations of antibiotics and human growth hormones. I cannot say why, but I see no danger.'

'Vigilance, brothers,' Zerberyn replied, unslinging his thunder hammer.

His predecessor had favoured the purist elegance of the power sword, but long before the moment he had been granted his pick of the Chapter armoury Zerberyn had known what he would select. The weapon was dormant in his grip, quiet, and would remain so until the moment of impact. And when that moment came, whatever it was on the end of it, Zerberyn meant for it to die. Such was the thunder hammer's pragmatic beauty.

Up close, the main door looked solid. Heavy plastek, proofed with an oily black sealant coating, hinged outwards and reinforced with armaplas crossbars. For an unmodified trooper, forcing access would have proven a complicated and time-consuming matter.

But not for him.

He dropped his pauldron plate and crashed his leading shoulder through without breaking stride. Shrugging off splinters, he straightened and scanned the room.

It was dark, cut off from the light of the stars and the ships massed in orbit, too dark even for the light-scavenging cells of his occulobe. His helm light beamed across riveted walls, ventilation grilles, moving onto a staircase against the left-side wall. The beam tracked it up to a mezzanine level, shadows of the square-sided balusters stretching out towards the rear wall and then angling sharply back across it as the beam moved on.

Hardran, Nalis and Borhune spread out, their own helmet beams dispersing through the cavernous space.

Zerberyn could hear murmuring, weeping, the strained sound of many, many bodies breathing. He sniffed. Even through his battleplate's rebreather apparatus he was getting the smell of something rancid.

His helm display busied his vision with floating markers. The position, facing, and condition of his squad showed as glowing gold numerals. Box reticules closed over objects of interest – an atmosphere conditioner, a swaying chain connected to some kind of overhead wash unit – furnishing them with a full tactical overlay of range, angles and threat recognition. Reticules floated against the dark, open, uncertain, as his helm light swept over a chain link enclosure.

Eyes glittered dully in the beam.

'What is it, brother?'

Tarsus. Zerberyn barely registered the vox-scratch in his ear. He grunted in disgust.

'Animals.'

FOURTEEN

Prax

The man looked up into the glare of Zerberyn's helmet beam with distant eyes. His pupils constricted to pinpricks and he recoiled from the light with a grunt, but did not otherwise appear to notice the giant in front of him. He was bruised, shorn, naked, but unusually fat. This was not the maltreatment Zerberyn would have expected from an alien conquerer. There was no brutality here. Injuries aside, which looked to be postural from remaining in one position for too long, rather than inflicted, the man looked as well-fed as any planetary governor.

Zerberyn moved his light on: blank faces luminesced under the beam, then returned to darkness and indignity as it passed. There must have been close to a hundred hemmed into the stall. There was no room for them to move, even to sit. The floor was perforated metal, for drainage, but the sheer volume of waste had clogged the pores and solid effluent heaped up in lumpen mounds over toes that were turning black with poor circulation and disease. The

stink was infernal. Despite everything that he was, Zerberyn felt himself back away. Slavery and squalor he had
encountered on many worlds. This was something other.
Something worse.

'There are more ahead,' called Nalis.

'Here also,' said Hardran, voice echoing from the stalls
away to the right.

'There must be thousands,' breathed Tosque, clumping
forwards from behind, tracking the creaking stillness of the
second level with his combi-plasma.

'Tens of thousands,' growled Columba.

Zerberyn spoke into his gorget pickup. 'Reoch. I need you
in here. Bring Brother Antille.'

An affirmative burred through his vox-channel. He killed
the squad frequency and looked around again, easing his
finger around the trigger of his pistol. Reticules wobbled
across his visor, searching for something to target.

'Detecting movement,' said Columba, his vox dialled
down to a low bass. He pointed up to the second floor.

'More stalls, perhaps,' said Zerberyn.

Columba shrugged.

'Hardran, search the upper level. Tosque, secure the stairs
and cover him. Nalis, run a circuit of the perimeter.'

The veteran-brothers nodded; in battleplate and deep
shadow it was an ominous, inhuman gesture. Apothecary
Reoch entered just as Nalis left. The glow of his binoptics
intensified as they adapted to the gloom. Antille ducked
through the splintered portico after him, vox antennae
twanging against the lintel beam.

Mendel Reoch meanwhile continued to the stalls.

There was a piston shock, flesh punctured, a breathless gasp.

The Apothecary's narthecium punched a sampler into the nearest captive's jugular. The man moaned piteously, legs wobbling, but the press of filthy bodies held him steady.

Zerberyn hovered his helm light over the man's gasping mouth, his curiosity piqued by something he had seen there. As well as having no hair, the man also had no teeth and, now he checked, no fingernails: nothing with which he could conceivably do harm to himself or another. A rare and unsettling cocktail of pity and disgust settled in his gut like one of Reoch's analgesic slimes. His roving beam paused on the face of a woman who opened her mouth placidly as though conditioned to associate light with water or food. There was something branded onto her cheek. Zerberyn moved closer. She remained as she was, mouth wide and waiting, even as Zerberyn enclosed her head in his gauntlet and turned it gently to the side.

The brand was that of a snake.

The man under Mendel Reoch's ministration gave one last grunt as the Apothecary's narthecium retracted.

'There are dangerously high levels of synthetic growth enhancers, testosterone, and other steroids in his blood. I would need to return him to *Dantalion*'s apothecarion for more thorough investigations.'

'Take him and one other and begin what tests you are able. I think we have what we came for. Raise the gunship,' Zerberyn added to Antille. 'We need evacuation for these two test subjects.'

'That deviates from the mission schematic, brother-captain.'

'The fault is ours,' said Zerberyn. 'We failed to anticipate the possibility of survivors. As you were ordered, brother.'

'Brother-captain!'

Straddling the top step and the next floor, Tosque swung his combi-plasma and helmet beam down onto whatever the veteran-brother had spotted amongst the stalls.

Zerberyn, Columba and Reoch instantly had pistols raised.

A human, unfettered and clothed, withered under the spotlight. Like his domesticated brethren, he was shorn and branded and denuded of teeth. Unlike them he had two off-white molars stapled into his brow. They reminded Zerberyn of rank pins, or the long-service studs that the veterans of other Chapters employed. The man licked his lips nervously, hugging a rusty pail to his chest as though to hide behind it. It slopped with a reddish-brown gelatin that Zerberyn initially hoped was waste but which, judging from the hanging mouths in the stalls to either side, he had the appalling suspicion was food.

The man bared his gums, squinting between Tosque and the others.

Then he screamed, shattering the night quiet like an intruder alarm.

It lasted half a second before mass-reactive rounds from four different weapons explosively ripped his body to pieces, vaporous parts of him filming the surrounding stalls.

The human cattle, mouths agape, began slowly to lick their lips.

Zerberyn held his breath as the echoes died. Chains and hoses clinked and swayed. Lips slurped. Tosque covered his angles warily. Columba calmly moved to cover another angle of approach through the maze of stalls. Zerberyn checked his visor display. Ident-runes shuffled across the display: there was Tarsus to his left, Galen and his team spreading out through the cattle sheds, Hardran in the plane above.

Nothing. He allowed his battle readiness to ease.

An enquiring grunt sounded from deeper in the complex. It was porcine, feral. Tension returned immediately to Zerberyn's grip. The battle for Eidolica was fresh in his memory, the savage grunt-speak of the alien a repugnance he would remember until death relieved him of his duty.

'Contacts!' he roared, stepping away from the stall and aiming his bolt pistol into the swaying, clinking, *snarling* dark.

His beam hit something green. Metal winked from an axe-blade, tooth caps, the lead-hued base of tribal body art. He spared a passing split-second of a thought to the human cattle all around, packed in so close he could feel their body heat. He dismissed the minor variable. There was no longer any hope for them.

He fired.

The bolt-round exploded in the ork's face, blasting the brute back and down against a partition wall. Reoch and Columba pushed forwards with him in lockstep, a perfect firing line, pistols blazing. From above, Tosque opened up with a strobing burst of fire, stitching a line of eviscerated ork green and human pink across a row of stalls. Without warning, the veteran-brother checked his fire, turned, and opened up on the second floor. Answering fire from stubbers and shooters bracketed the Space Marine's armour and chewed into the steel wall behind him. He held firm, breaking up the incoming fire with controlled, even bursts of bolter fire.

A triumphant cry filled the unit vox, then cut off. Hardran's rune blinked from gold to black in Zerberyn's visor. Red threat icons, generated by his suit's auspex, boiled around the edges of his display.

A firecrack bang hit the side of his helm with something hot and wet.

He staggered back until his genetic gifts could eliminate the aural shock and reassert his sense of balance. Reoch was down, a bullet in his temple. Zerberyn stepped over the downed Apothecary, solid slugs spanking off his battleplate.

Heavy stubber fire was thundering down on him from the second level. By weight of numbers and brute resilience, a mob of orks had taken the overhang that looked over the factory floor and forced Tosque onto the stairs. The veteran was firing point-blank now, descending backwards, ceding the stair step by step.

The orks were huge, bare-chested, arrogant in their simplicity. In a moment of clarity, Zerberyn saw them for what they were. They were the greenskins' exemplars.

With a furious cry, Columba fired up his chainsword. The sergeant stepped up onto the air-cycler set against the stair-side wall and jumped across the walkspace, reaching the opposite side stall where he kicked, a servo-assisted release of superhuman force that drove his power-armoured bulk crashing through the metal balustrades and into the orks piling down the stairs. Blood sprayed across the wall, and for a moment it was impossible to distinguish the howls of the orks from that of Columba's chainsword.

Reoch's mouth-grille chewed out gravel sounds as he shook his head and rose with a slur of motorised joints, freeing a frag grenade from the clutch at his hip. He pulled the pin and lobbed the charge overarm onto the second level.

The explosion blew out the handrail, smashed the orks' lacklustre fire discipline and brought down part of the ceiling. The Apothecary turned his half-metal grimace on Zerberyn. His face was a bloody mess, the bullet trapped between the metallic struts that secured his augmetics to the bone.

'Retrograde aberrations,' he snarled.

Zerberyn yanked the Apothecary behind him as an ork wearing serpentine tattoos and what looked like human-skin shorts kicked through a stall door and charged. Its axe clanged against Zerberyn's raised vambrace. Steel on cer-amite, it never stood a chance. With a loud crack the haft splintered, the head spinning aside, but the strength behind the initial blow was phenomenal and sent Zerberyn reeling.

A bolt-round punched through the ork's ribcage and blasted half its chest out through its back. A second round blew out the other half before a third in quick succession detonated between its eyes and finally killed it in its tracks. Brother Antille lowered his boltgun, the muzzle steaming hot.

'Gunship inbound. Five minutes.'

Zerberyn nodded gratitude and opened a vox-link. 'Pull back to the landing zone and regroup.' He turned to Reoch.

'Select your subjects, Apothecary. They are to be the lucky ones after all.'

The bloodied Apothecary lowered his pistol and stalked to the nearest stall to obey.

Antille hefted his boltgun to cover Reoch while Zerberyn slowly backed up, laying down fire to enable Tosque and Columba to break away and withdraw. A resounding clang pulled Zerberyn's attention back towards Reoch and Antille.

A ventilator grille banged against the wall and a double-jointed runt of a creature, the serf caste called gretchin, slid on its backside out of the shaft. There, it freed up the stubber in its lap and let rip on full-auto. Ricochets sprang between Reoch and Antille's heavy battleplate, but the runt's aim was not nearly so discriminate. The bullet spray perforated the stall partition and several men and women took hits. They mewled like stricken animals, unable even to fall over as they died.

Zerberyn dragged the creature out by the head and crushed its skull with a mild application of force.

Reoch, a bald, plump female over one pauldron and a male over the other, indicated that he was ready.

Columba and Tosque joined them, the latter raking what was left of the second level with suppressive fire while the sergeant, grey plate a gory black, squeezed off snapshots at anything that so much as threatened to be green.

The four Space Marines formed a closed cage around the Apothecary, the orks hurling themselves against the wall made by the sons of Dorn and finding it unbreakable.

'Out,' Zerberyn yelled over the doubled thunder of bolter

fire, anchoring the retreat as, one by one, his brothers followed Reoch out.

Exiting one firestorm, and entering another.

FIFTEEN

Prax

Orks crowded the agri-plex's windows and chutes, pumping the loading yard between the buildings with high-calibre shot. Crude rocket-propelled grenades screamed through the air like kamikaze bombers and blew great spumes of earth from the road. Zerberyn and his brothers gathered around Reoch and his charges and returned fire, picking their targets, always retreating towards the landing zone. An off-spherical grenade crashed through the corrugated roof of one of the cattle sheds and gutted it with fire. Zerberyn raised his arm against the pelting shrapnel and tried to instil some sense into what had happened to his battlefield.

The fighting was too intense and widespread to be the work of his squad alone, and if the Iron Warriors had entered the field then he would surely know about it.

He could see Brother Tarsus. The veteran was firing from behind the thick metal legs of the water tank, minimising himself as a visible target. Brother Donbuss and his heavy bolter, meanwhile, were still watching over the landing zone, outdoing the orks' combined firepower both for sheer destructiveness and for noise. The belt-fed torrent of high-explosive anti-personnel rounds left twisted metal and pulverised plate wherever the orks sought to establish a firebase.

Karva announced his presence some distance to the right amongst the slurry tanks with the mighty whoomph of his heavy flamer. An expanding mushroom of promethium wash sent burning debris pattering onto the surrounding roofs like hailstones. Glottal shouts and more crude gunfire answered back. Staccato bursts. So far, so well enough within the mission schematic that Zerberyn had established during descent. At the same time as those flames were dying back however, a flurry of las supercharged to the red end of the energy spectrum spat between various silos, and even from the dust desert that surrounded the oasis of rusted tin and steel.

There was movement beneath the wind turbines.

Human troopers in moulded black carapace and dust-bowl fatigues were hurrying towards the main structure, providing rolling overwatch. Another two squads, twenty men and support weaponry, advanced more deliberately through the silos, flushing out lone orks and gretchin workers ahead of them with grenades and disciplined volleys of hot-shot. Zerberyn had seen skitarii units move like that. One will, one intent. For what looked like unaugmented human soldiers, their unit discipline was exemplary.

A mechanised growl pulled Zerberyn's attention to the ramshackle ork tractor in the machine shed that he had marked on his initial approach.

With a trembling of its rust-brown frame, it powered back out of the shed at speed. It lurched into a handbrake spin, flat tyres skidding up dust, tarpaulin roof ballooning, then jumped forwards. There was an ork at the wheel, a dark-skinned patriarch with a leather eye patch and a massive jaw, firing one-handed out of the driver's side window with a twin-linked stubber. A gang of squealing gretchin packed the rear container, holding on to the metal sides or to the single ladder that ran up the back, and blazed wildly in all directions. A bullet punched a trooper from his feet, reflex pulling a wild burst of las skyward as he fell. His squadmates spread out into the thin cover of the various silos and raked the careening vehicle with las-fire.

A fireball lit off under the truck's rear exhaust, flipping the vehicle over and into a roll that ended with it on its side and white with dust.

'Beautiful,' said Columba, drilling a dazed-looking gretchin that staggered from the up-ended rear compartment with a bolt-round.

Zerberyn shot his gaze back towards the silos and the unexpected aid streaming from them. An officer and his bodyguard were running towards Zerberyn's position, heads down, while the remaining troopers laid down suppressive fire.

On approaching the towering Fists Exemplar captain, the officer pulled himself straight, transferred the second of the two hellpistols he was carrying to his off-hand, and threw a sharp salute. Half the fingers of his hand had been replaced with augmetics. The horror of burned flesh that had cost him that side of his face and eyesight was old enough to have scarred and yet looked to have received little or no medicae attention.

'Major Dannat Bryce. Seventeenth Gammic Dragoons.' He spoke in an easy yell that carried his voice over the explosive chatter of gunfire. His damaged face glowed, flushed with supreme self-righteousness and the Emperor's love. 'And as pleased as you might expect to see you here, my lord.'

'Astra Militarum?' asked Zerberyn.

Bryce gave what was, by its own unfortunate necessity, a crooked smile. 'You have something that needs doing, you call on the Astra Militarum. You have something that needs *done* then you call for the Seventeenth.'

'Militarum Tempestus,' muttered Columba. 'Scions. There was a battalion of them deployed to the compliance campaign on Crantar Seven.'

'We spotted two more gunships, one from another Chapter,' said one of the major's guards earnestly. A big man, only a foot or so shorter than Zerberyn, and from the weight of his gear some kind of mission specialist. Zerberyn guessed ordnance. 'Are they hitting other targets? When can we expect the rest of the liberation fleet?'

'You're out of line, sergeant,' snapped Bryce, then turned to Zerberyn with an apologetic shrug. 'We've been a long time outside of chain of command, my lord.'

'How long?'

'I lose track. Several months. We're here on a Commissariat Special Objective – slow the orks down in whatever way we can and prepare the ground for reconquest. Weren't you informed?'

'Months?' said Zerberyn, ignoring the question. 'Then you can tell us about the orks' activities here.'

'We could. Do you have time for a detour?'

'We have time.'

'Then we can show you. There's an orbital command substation twelve hours east of here as you head towards Princus Praxa.'

'Advise that we explain on the way,' barked a female trooper with the coarse voice of a lho-stick lifer and the frosty exterior of an ice world. She was looking at the slate monitorum set into the back of her left gauntlet. It showed what appeared to be heat sources over a grid. A solid mass of them were congregating directly ahead, while still more continued to spill in from the edges. 'The orks are regrouping inside the agri-plex, and Sergeant Cullen reports two vehicle squadrons inbound with flyer support.'

Bryce turned questioningly to Zerberyn, who nodded. They could spare another twelve hours. And he could already hear the sound of approaching engines. He doubted whether they could all be extracted by air before ork reinforcements arrived, and he would be loath to leave a useful force of Imperial soldiery to the captivity of the greenskins. The human chattel currently held within the agri-plex were another matter. They were, he had concluded, a neutral variable, neither an asset to the success of his mission nor a hindrance, and could thus most usefully be ignored.

'Antille,' Zerberyn voxed. 'Contact Kalkator and inform him of the change in plan. Tell him to be quick, we have ork aircraft inbound.'

'As you say, brother.'

Zerberyn removed his helmet with a hiss of demagnetisation and focused his hearing on the incoming petrochem growl, his Lyman's ear isolating it from the din and sharpening it.

It was the distant but rapidly closing roar of a Thunderhawk's combat engines.

Zerberyn looked up at the moment that the Iron Warriors gunship *Meratara* came down behind the line of wind turbines, losing itself in the dust thrown up by its underwing exhausts. The bi-blades spun until they blurred, droning, superfast, chips of metallic debris spanking off the blades. Turbofans angling to hover, the gunship's box jaw pivoted towards the agri-plex and opened up with its full forward arsenal.

Zerberyn cursed, shoved Bryce to the ground and crouched over him.

'Defend the Apothecary!'

Turbo-lasers, heavy bolters and lascannons chewed through the structure with a sound like a woodsaw biting on steel. Men and transhumans alike broke from combat and threw themselves down as a quartet of hellstrike missiles whistled from the Thunderhawk's underwing hardpoints and into the agri-plex. Explosions blossomed along the building's width, spread low like demolition charges rigged, primed and detonated in sequence, triggering a chain collapse that brought its metal walls crashing into dust and fire.

Zerberyn, still crouched protectively over the lightly concussed Tempestus Scions commander, turned his face into the heat storm. Bits of metal and burning cinders streamed down like a scene from the last days of the Siege. Massive warriors, veterans in ornate gunmetal and bronze, moved through the pyroclastic rain and brought bolters to bear.

'Arise, little cousin,' said Kalkator.

The warsmith's deep voice resonated harshly from the

glowing vox-grille of his horned helmet. His baroque Mark III power armour was embellished with hooks strung with barbed wire, weird devices, and campaign citations from a hundred worlds rendered lifeless by war a millennium before Zerberyn had been born. His left arm was a bionic of superb integration and design, the product of a craft lost to all but a few.

Dazed, Bryce looked from one Space Marine to the other, his mouth making confused, soundless shapes.

The twin barrels of Kalkator's combi-bolter were trained between Zerberyn's eyes.

'My gunship has room enough for your squad. Take what you came for and leave before the orks come back for vengeance.'

'You are a soulless traitor, Kalkator. There were people in there.'

'It is a war of survival we fight. I wage it as though it is one I intend to win. We received your update, were you not about to abandon them?'

'There is a difference. Your own survival, I am convinced you treasure. But not mine, nor theirs.'

Zerberyn pointed to the Scions scattered about. A good number had gone to ground amongst the battered silos as soon as the agri-plex had gone up and most of them had visual augmenter beams dancing over the Iron Warrior's armour. Had the Imperium seen fit to educate even its best with a fuller knowledge of its history and its foes, then things would have become very ugly very fast.

'Truer words were never uttered by a bastard of Dorn,' said Kalkator. 'But at this moment my fate is dependent on yours.'

'Our mission is unfinished. These men speak of an operation of some kind being conducted on the surface nearby, a data trove of the orks' activities that is within our grasp if we can move faster than word of our presence here.'

'Arise,' Kalkator growled again. His gauntlet finger slid across his combi-bolter's trigger like a whetstone over a sickle. 'I will kill these men before they can lead you to your death.'

'You would have to kill me to do it.'

'Do you think you would be the first?'

Zerberyn met the ruby glare of the warsmith's gaze without fear.

The Iron Warrior grunted with frustration and lowered his weapon. Even for a near-immortal, transhuman monster like Kalkator, time was finite and precious – as rare as an ally.

'The gods curse you, you and the stubbornness of your stock. Very well, we will go with you one step further. Apothecary,' he barked at Reoch. 'You may keep your cargo aboard my gunship for safekeeping.'

Zerberyn's triumphant smile faded.

Through the dust sent rolling out from underneath the Thunderhawk's idling turbofans, there came the rolling snarl of engines. Headlamps pierced the cloud, and for a heart-stilling moment Zerberyn thought that the orks' relief force was on them already, but then the slab-sided gunmetal shapes of a squadron of Iron Warriors bikers drove snarling through the murk. Wide rubber tyres with deep, spiked treads chewed the loose ground as they took position by the wind turbines.

Behind them marched a second ten-man squad, who fanned out, adopting a staggered firing line of bolters and siege weaponry, shielding the ponderous advance of a final three Iron Warriors behind them. They were huge, armoured like tanks, and bound in razor wire. Terminators. The colossi stomped into position behind the Traitor Space Marines, Tactical Dreadnought suits purring and belching black smoke as they redressed the aim of their combi-bolters towards the Militarum Tempestus men.

Zerberyn's smile returned as he found himself oddly pleased by this restoration of a cosmic truth.

'One squad each, is it?'

'As your precious Codex tells you, little cousin: if your enemy has one squad, bring two.'

SIXTEEN

Mars – Pavonis Mons

Nictitating membranes flickered across the empty, machined eyes of Zeta-One Prime. It was the cold, infinitely patient stare of a reptile, a chamaeleonidae watching a fly. Urquidex tried to abstract her from his consciousness, but the cold sense of her silver presence on the back of his neck was an order of magnitude worse. He shivered and pulled up the collar of his robe. Presumably, the skitarius' build had been designed to elicit exactly that kind of biological response. Cold-blooded to warm. Predator, prey.

He glanced up from the half-translated cartogenetic instructional he had been reading line by line from storage wafers into the data reliquary. At least, that was mostly what he had been doing.

Genetic readers rumbled as they worked at their endless task, laser diffraction painting the eddying smoke with hazy lines of rainbow colours. The thudding steps of laboratorium servitors and the lilt of chanting hung with the dry fumes. A pair of initiate adepts drifted through it, there but, in some crucially contextual way, elsewhere, red-robed ghosts of flesh and cabling.

Zeta-One Prime was the only thing that was still. She stood while Urquidex sat, watching, her arc pistol holstered under her hand.

'What are you doing?' she asked suddenly.

'I am instructing the cognis units to equivalate sequence and textual data with galactic grid references.'

'Again?'

'It must be done each time. The repetition is important.'

The skitarius fell silent a moment.

'The first time you performed this task it required fifteen minutes and eleven seconds. You have been at this terminal for sixteen minutes, magos.'

With an effort, Urquidex suppressed the anxious tic of his digitools. They made him look guilty. The skitarius' membranes flickered, some kind of sub-binaric code familiar to the deep biologics of his hindbrain.

I know.

He swallowed, tasted acid.

'How much longer will this task require?'

'I...' He glanced at the reliquary's scratchy, chrome-edged rune display, the lines of machine code that, though he could comprehend barely one symbol in five, he still knew betrayed a lot more than a cartogenetic instructional. He was resting a great deal on the faith that no mere skitarius, however elevated, would have been initiated into the First Circle of Information. 'Two minutes.'

'You have one.'

'But–'

'The artisan trajectorae apprised me of your sub-optimal performance in your prior duty designation. I will not tolerate the same here.'

'But–'

'Fifty-two seconds, magos.'

Biting his tongue and begging the machine's clemency for such discourteous haste, he recited the final lines of the instructional via the data reliquary's stiff ivory keys. As he worked, his digitools slid indepently over the tiers of keys.

'*I am close.*'

The runes hovered in the machine's active buffer, the noospheric equivalent of short term memory, for about five seconds before the detailed instructional he was inputting with his other hand swept them away.

'*How close?*'

The question illuminated the electronic firmament. The data-strings were inelegantly composed, the syntax of quantum bits crude and, though the final form was legible, evidence of an inexpert hand.

But Clementina Yendl was no adept.

It had only taken a few days after his transfer from Noctis Labyrinth for her to locate him once more, and though Van Auken's laboratorium was too well isolated for them to meet in person, they communicated. From her he had learned of the orks over Terra and more, sensed the urgency of her cause in the haste with which she 'spoke'. He had not asked who she really was or whom she really served. Perhaps because the experience of trusting another person, of believing in their cause, was too precious to risk with such questions.

'*Three days,*' he sent back. '*Two days if I do not purge the prognosticators of scrapcode, but the accuracy of our results will suffer.*'

'*If you had to leave Mars now, could you finish?*'

'Now?'

'Magos?' said Zeta-One Prime, making him start.

He had not intended to speak aloud.

'Stand by,' he said, trying to make a dry mouth sound confident.

Disconnecting from the data reliquary, he hurried through the whirring stacks of cogitators. The kick of his robes disturbed ankle-deep engine smoke. His heart was pounding though he wasn't sure why. A fly being watched by a chamaeleonidae.

Surrounded by trembling apparatus, a quiescent hololith table gave off a stilted glow. Urquidex connected himself through a series of peripheral nervous plugs. His fingers were sweating and it took several tries.

He was aware of Zeta-One Prime watching. For now, just watching. This action was abnormal, and the abnormal made her wary.

With a sympathetic impulse, he bade the hololith to awaken.

A three-dimensional map of the Imperium of Man shimmered into being. To his telescopic optics it was a heat map, data-dense regions showing through as yellows and reds, spiral arms separated by dark bands of nothing. Urquidex willed the data-vision to change. Hotspots and stellar landmarks dispersed, to be replaced by the branching lines of a phylogenetic tree. Except that 'tree' was too fleshbound a metaphor. Two-dimensional. It was more like the growth of a bacterial colony on a nutrient plate or the filamentous spread of a fungus. Offshoots extended into every segmentum of Imperial space, expanding outwards in three dimensions from a common root somewhere in the galactic core. The data represented it as an amorphous zone, grey and ill-defined, unpleasing on the diligent eye. The uncertainties were being continually smoothed away as the sequence mapping progressed, but it still covered hundreds of light years of congested space, thousands of worlds. His own cortex might be capable of processing it. He shook his head.

It was too complex.

'Install a high capacity cable-link between the hololith and the data reliquary.'

'To what purpose?'

'Because I require it,' Urquidex snapped, heart fumbling, and then with what he prayed was proper urgency rather than panic, 'Please. Every second increases the likelihood of data degradation.'

He was aware of the interlink the instant that it was made. It was an erupting singularity of blinding connectivity, light and sound, thought and sensation, that even through the remove of a peripheral plug-in was almost overwhelming. He shunted the upload to a cortical machine sub-consciousness and did his best to disregard it.

'*The orks originate somewhere in the galactic core. It is a dense area. It will take time to isolate the exact world.*'

Silence from the machine. The data galaxy spiralled, spiralled.

'*Yendl?*'

Nothing.

'This deviates, magos,' said Zeta-One Prime, overcoming a pre-programmed fear of these machines and their workings with obvious reluctance. 'If there is a problem then I am obligated to inform the artisan trajectorae.'

'No. There is no need for that.'

He looked up.

The skitarius was up close: not angry, she was incapable of that, but as anxious as her emotional clamps allowed her to be. She radiated an artifical cold that needled around Urquidex's implants and into the bone. Behind her, a woman in plain red robes approached. An initiate adept with a data-slate for inspection.

Odd.

The initiates worked on independent projects. They had never reported to him before.

The crack of a las discharge rang out like a hammer striking a nail. Zeta-One Prime jerked forward. There was another shot and she stumbled into the hololith, making the image shake. Ionised smoke uncoiling from the las-burns to her silvery exoskeleton, she began to turn.

The initiate struck her across the face with the data-slate. The slate bent in two in an eruption of sparks and knocked the skitarius back into the projector. A sharp kick into the shin dropped her onto her knees. A laspistol came up in the initate's other hand and pushed up against the back of Zeta-One Prime's skull. With laser clarity, Urquidex noted that the selector had been switched to full auto.

The skitarius' head lit up like a soldering iron and she

slumped to the ground, head slagged and fused to her shoulders.

A blurt of interrogative binaric came from behind the cogitator stacks and the second initiate came running.

The first was already dropping, minimising her profile even as she cast aside her emptied laspistol and with mercuric grace drew Zeta-One Prime's arc pistol. The running initiate was armed with basic digital weaponry and spat low-powered laser bolts from his extended arm as soon as he spotted the fallen skitarius. They all missed.

The female took her moment, aimed and then fired. A crackling fist of electricity punched the initiate from his feet and slammed him into the brass cladding of a codifier.

Urquidex gaped.

'Not later,' said Clementina Yendl, manually tearing his plug-ins from the hololith projector. The abrupt separation was as extraordinary as the connection had been, and almost wiped him out with pain.

'Now.'

SEVENTEEN

Prax

The orbital command substation was an immense agglomeration of cylindrical towers dish arrays and landing platforms that in better days would have serviced light jurisdictional compliance craft responsible for inspection and enforcement of orbital traffic. The facility was surrounded by a crumpled wire fence, and was all just within sight of Princus Praxa's outer walls. The city was a thumb's-width smudge on the horizon, a coppery pall of particulate pollution that glimmered like living crystal from the final-stage escape boosters of orbital lifters.

The orks, as Major Bryce had explained it, utilised the substation's communication nets to complement their own orbital operations.

Zerberyn could have inferred that much for himself from the sheer concentration of firepower that the orks had embedded there in its defence.

Pot-bellied howitzers thrust out of sandbagged redoubts. For such large, crude-looking artillery pieces they had a tremendous rate of fire, thumping out explosive shells and sending up rockets of dusty topsoil amidst the Fists Exemplar advance. Machine cannons screamed as they ripped up new trenchlines.

Scrap metal drizzled over Zerberyn's armour. Dust clogged the glowing lenses of his helm.

The bombardment was a variable that, having already plotted the optimal angle of attack at the onset, he could no longer influence and so spared no further thought to.

A combat squad comprising one-half of Veteran Squad Anatoq moved with him over the broken ground in a line, their even spacing the resultant practical of Brother Donbuss' best theoretical of the howitzer shells' blast radius. The five Space Marines were flickering gold auspex traces in Zerberyn's faceplate display, periodically broken up by dust diffraction and blast compression fronts. They fired sporadically, conserving ammunition, the soundless flashes of muzzle-flare in the cacophony primarily to give the orks something to aim at other than the true source of the attack.

With their genhanced low-light vision and complementary auspex overlays bolstering their awareness, the Fists Exemplar guided the lighter Tempestus Scions in. Patched in to the humans' platoon frequency, Zerberyn listened in on their chatter as he picked a path through the stick bombs, tube-charges and tripwires that his auto-senses' threat-recognition protocols called out from the general detritus.

Even had these men been Space Marines, Zerberyn would have been impressed by their vox-discipline. There was none of the braggadocio and backchat that he was accustomed to hearing on mortal units' channels. Just target advisories, calm requests for recharge packs or medicae assistance, and mapping updates that were followed immediately and without question. Zerberyn had not yet seen the Scions truly tested, but if they achieved nothing else today then they had already accomplished a feat that was practically unheard of.

They had impressed an Exemplar.

'Unidentified heat source on your eleven,' voxed one, their system clear as a bell.

The heat source saw Zerberyn the moment that Zerberyn saw it, and fired a moment later. A Devil Dog flame tank, hull down and scarred enough by battle-damage to justify Zerberyn's initial appraisal that it had been derelict. An ork in an ill-fitting flak jacket and a red bandana lifted its head above the hatch and shouted.

He would submit himself for proper penance when the battle was done.

A melta beam lanced from its turret gun in a howl of deconstituted atmosphere and passed a foot over Zerberyn's shoulder, incinerating half of the following Scions in an instant. Heat washed over him. He hit the ground, rolling into the cover formed by the scrap and craters surrounding the substation as the tank's glacis-mounted heavy bolter opened up.

'Mine, *cousin.*'

An Iron Warriors Terminator strode directly into the firing line. His monstrous battleplate soaked up the glacis-mount's magazine as mass-reactive rounds from his own combi-bolter spanked across the Devil Dog's gunner slit. A disruption field thrummed into life around the clenched fingers of his power fist as the Cataphractii disappeared again into the fog of war.

'Tarsus, Galen – pincer left,' voxed Zerberyn, rising and clapping dust from his bolt pistol. 'Tosque, Nalis, Borhune: right.'

His squad knew their duties, but it always paid to keep their wiser-than-thou individualism in check.

'Jaskólska,' he went on, switching to the Scions' channel, addressing the female trooper he had spoken with briefly at the agri-plex. 'We have you covered.'

'Our gratitude, lord captain.'

The surviving Scions, no grief, no complaint, took off at a full sprint. They were bug-eyed by the full covering and rebreather apparatus of their omnishield helms. The greenish glow of visual augmenter beams from their hell-gun scopes webbed the air like a haywired security grid.

Zerberyn followed, finding the troopers spread out in a semicircular firebase formation, Sergeant Jaskólska and the unit sapper in the process of mag-locking the final melta bombs to the substation's Dreadnought-sized main doors.

'Clear!' yelled the sapper with considerable, long pent-up satisfaction, and then activated the det-charges via his slate monitorum.

White fire rolled out from the doors with a searing roar. Zerberyn felt a passing discomfort in his eyes before his auto-senses adapted to the supernova glare and filtered out the more damaging wavelengths. He was stepping into the breach with weapons ready while the Scions still had their arms over their helms' visors.

The gunmetal floor tiles glittered like a starfield, littered with flakes of glass that a moment ago had been dust. Opposite, a security desk sat behind a reinforced shatter-glass screen, the window turned almost completely white with cracks. On various walls, the torn corner scraps of instructional posters fluttered as the vestibule breathed in, exchanging the oxygen that the melta bombs had consumed for smoke from outside.

He shot and killed an ork that pushed its way in through an interior door, then another, and another. Shot, kill; shot kill. Purity through utility.

More were coming, discernably different from the savage fighters he had encountered on Prax thus far. Another greenskin sub-type, perhaps. Another *clan*. Their alien features were encased in horned helms, obscene musculature clad in thick body armour decorated with an optically striking black-and-white checker pattern. There were too many, and the number of entrance corridors was too great, for even transhuman reflexes and Space Marine armament to hold them at bay.

Zerberyn swung his thunder hammer as he charged headlong into the pack. The timed-release detonation vaporised the first ork's torso, pasted its legs in two long red streaks back the way it had come, and lifted the half-tonne brute behind it off its feet, sending it crashing through the shatterglass screen. Another, hard and green and slabbed in armour, came in across his swing. It roared, all aggression. He roared back, vox-amplified to a crippling pitch, as the ork slammed into his turned shoulder and bulldozed him into the wall.

Nalis and Borhune arrived in a storm of bolter fire that shredded the ork. Following in their wake came Jaskólska and her Scions, lighting up the room with full-auto bursts of hot-shot las. Powerful though the Scions' hellguns were compared to the standard Guardsman's lasrifle, each monstrous greenskin took several point-blank blasts to put down, and several more to finish off.

The last ork crunched onto the glass-strewn tiles, crisped like meat held too long against the heat.

Zerberyn disinterred himself from the dented wall and opened a channel.

'Columba, Major.' He masked the twitch of his lip and swallowed his distaste. 'Kalkator. Entrance secured. See that the perimeter is held and join me in the control room.'

'A pity our fathers were such adversaries,' voxed Kalkator. 'Together, their sons would have been unstoppable.'

'In some other universe, perhaps,' Zerberyn returned, and then, aware that Bryce was also on the channel, added a poisonous, '*cousin.*'

That was an explanation that he did not want to have to give. Not now. And not to Marshal Bohemond when they finally rejoined the muster at Phall.

He scowled.

First Captain Zerberyn of the Fists Exemplar did not answer to the Black Templars.

'This facility's data stores had better be worth it.'

'This way, lord captain,' said Jaskólska smartly, unaware that the warning had been intended for himself.

Glass ground under her feet as she eased open an interior door and stepped over the greenskin corpse that had been holding it ajar. Zerberyn followed, then Nalis, Borhune, Tosque and Galen. Tarsus remained behind to hold the vestibule, directing the remaining Scions into fire points behind upturned tables and security lockers.

A short corridor led to a metal staircase. It looked like something that would have been used by lower-grade servants and perhaps as an escape route during emergency drills. Access doors onto exterior walkways stood on each tier, bloody handprints on the emergency release bars. A pair of panicked-looking gretchin came clattering down the escape and straight into two precise blasts from Jaskólska's hellgun. They rolled down, the sounds of bolter fire ringing back through the stairwell's metal frame as Zerberyn and the major pushed through another door and into a control room.

The terminals were still active, continuing with their operators *in absentia* to plot the blips and curves of an intensely crowded near-orbital space. Empty, bloodstained chairs were set up along curving desks, blinking, chirping workstations facing an armourglass window. The view was of an endless beige plain of desertified pastureland. A railroad cut across it, trailed by a dust road. Both ran from the substation to Princus Praxa. Zerberyn manually operated his helm's magnification selector. It was no substitute for a pair of magnoculars, but it bought him a blurry three- or four-fold zoom – enough to make out the mottled grey industrial stacks crowding the city's outer walls. The chimneys pumped out a grimy, ochre smog that hazed almost everything else within it. Even the high adamantium-ceramite walls of the Crusade-era citadel that dominated the settlement's heart were little more than a gothic, crimson shadow.

'What is that smoke?'

'The people of Prax,' said Major Bryce, appearing in the door ahead of Columba and Kalkator and a handful of Scions. 'And a billion more from off-world, brought here to be... rendered.'

Zerberyn turned from the window as Columba strode past. The veteran-sergeant ignored the panorama entirely, thumped through the glazed metal doors onto the main staircase, and then blazed down the corridor with his bolt pistol to a riot of high-pitched screams. Kalkator joined Zerberyn at the glass. Jaskólska moved warily aside, some deep conditioning of her training causing her to half-raise her hellgun and slip behind a desk. The Iron Warrior disengaged his helmet's seals and removed it, nose wrinkling as he took it under his arm and gazed across the plain towards the fortress that Perturabo had built. His eyes were pained, distant, his primarch's glories dust.

'You have seen it?' said Zerberyn to the major.

'Throne, have I seen it,' muttered Bryce, hugging his carapace as though the armourglass provided no protection against the winds of the plain. 'The smell of the tanneries stays on you for days, and the screams of the children...'

'You are only human. It is understandable.'

Bryce nodded, grateful for that. He pointed to a humming stack of cogitator units that stood against the wall behind a clear plastek barrier. 'The data-cache.'

'I am no priest of Mars, major.'

'I suggest we pull up the unit and take it with us, First Captain.' Brother Antille walked over, shadowed by the smaller form of Bryce's vox-officer-cum-adjutant, Sergeant Menthis, and greeted Zerberyn with a curt nod. 'I can bear the weight, and see it safely loaded aboard the gunship. Once we return to *Dantalion* Forge-Brother Clathrin can conduct the necessary rites of retrieval.'

'Do it.'

'Everything the orks have done from here will have been automatically stored by the system,' said Bryce. 'Thousands of ships take off and land every day, and even more are unloaded from orbit. You'll be able to learn what the orks are doing from that, I have no doubt.'

'I can tell you what the orks are doing,' said Kalkator, turning his nailhead stare on Zerberyn, ignoring the Scion utterly. 'They are feeding an empire.'

Zerberyn looked again at that crimson pall. As if the thermosphere wept blood. If his transhuman biology had retained the ability for him to be physically sick, then he would have been so. By the Emperor's wisdom, he was forced to keep his disgust internal; it stewed in his gut, suffused him, a familiar outrage trembling in the marrow of his bones.

Feed.

'You saw the number of ships in orbit, little cousin,' said Kalkator. 'The industry of Prax could be supplying offensives against hundreds of sectors.'

'What are you suggesting?'

'You know what I am suggesting.'

'You did not want to be on this planet. Now you are talking of reconquering it.'

'Orks do not settle, they burn. They took no prisoners on Ostrom or Klostra or on Eidolica. I could not have known that *this* would be here.'

'There must be ten thousand orks in that city, defending a Fourth Legion citadel. There is no combination of variables that can sum forty men and fewer than thirty Adeptus Astartes into a schema of victory.'

With a scowl, Kalkator replaced his helm over his head. His armour resealed with a clank of magnetic clamps. The next words he spoke came directly through Zerberyn's helmet channel.

'Forget the citadel. The fortress is but the surface of a complex of subterranean bunkers that runs beneath the entire city. The entrances are concealed and gene-locked. We can take the citadel, and hold it long enough for our ships to land additional forces to cleanse the planet.'

Zerberyn closed his eyes and considered. The parameters of the modified mission schematic would recommend utilising the substation's communications and landing capability to apprise the fleet and call down Thunderhawk extraction to remove the data-cache to safety, and then most likely destroy the facility on their departure. But there was merit to Kalkator's argument. He opened his eyes and met the warsmith's glowing, red-lensed stare.

That horned mask was hiding something, he felt certain, but the Iron Warrior was too altered from his exalted origins, his manner too void of humanity, for him to guess what.

'We need only get into the city,' said Kalkator.

Zerberyn's eyes followed the line of the railroad, across the plain and into Princus Praxa's bleak industrial heart.

There was merit.

He nodded, feeling an adrenal buzz suffuse his muscles as his body prepared itself for the combat promised by that red horizon. It felt good.

The fightback began now.

EIGHTEEN

Terra – the Imperial Palace

The Praetorian Way was the primary arterial between Anterior Six Gate and the Great Chamber. Fortified senatorial habs and basilicae soared above like mountains, bristling with rusted autocannon turrets and the roosts of angels, their stone faces teared by acid corrosion. Lumen globes mounted on posts lined the way, glittering like an honour guard drawn from the span of the Imperium. Brass filters shaped the light into continents and oceans, each a commemoration to the world of an Army regiment destroyed in defence of Terra. Kilometre after kilometre, they stood vigil against the deepening twilight. Lord High Admiral Lansung had intended to climax his victory march here following the Navy's triumph at Vesperilles, and over the course of the Siege both loyalists and traitors had exploited the arterial to move their war machines between inner and outer Palace.

Now it was locked down.

Barriers and visored enforcers stood on the ramps and slip roads. Like clockwork, a black Adeptus Arbites armoured transport would cruise down the centre lane with exhortations to good order and obedience booming from its loudspeakers.

It was a rare sight then, if not an unprecedented one, when a squadron of Imperial Fists Land Raiders roared onto the flyway.

They pulled away from the towers, moving in convoy. The cut light sharpened angular lines to a golden edge. The immense power of their engines rumbled into the angels' eyries above, and ruffled the forever-twilight of the ornamental canopy of the Night Garden below.

The Land Raider was a beast of war, one of unique inelegance in the armouries of the Angels of Death, but unrivalled in the execution of its singular function. The bonded layers of its composite armour were as near to impenetrable as the artifice of man could make them, the tank front-loaded with firepower and battlefield superiority. It was the ground-to-ground equivalent of a drop pod or a boarding torpedo, its role to deliver Space Marines into the violent, still-beating heart of battle with crushing force. Its armour, armament and machine temperament suited it equally to rolling over troops, armour and even the fortifications of an enemy in order to gain its target.

The lead vehicle pulled up before the gilded stone portal of the Senatorum Imperialis.

Sponson lascannons tracked back and forth over the imposing defensive structure as two more vehicles rolled out alongside it. The fourth and last, an ultra-rare example of the siege-breaking Achilles variant, heaved to a stop behind the other tanks. Its hull-mounted thunderfire cannon and sponson multi-meltas zeroed in on the gate.

The Imperial Fists were dead. Ardamantua had ended them. But their serfs, the *Phalanx*, their Chapter houses here on Terra, their armouries, vaults and frozen gene-stocks – all still remained. The Chapter was mustering its strength for one last, defiant shout.

The Achilles revved its engines, wrecking-ball frame leaning into its forward brakes.

Its ultimatum was explicit.

The Lucifer Blacks lieutenant in command of the guard detail appeared in the embrasure window of the guardroom above the gate. His hand was clamped to an earpiece and he was speaking urgently into a wired vox-unit mounted on the guardroom wall.

Koorland popped the cupola hatch of the Achilles, then stepped off the roof of the tank and onto the road. Chapter serfs in gold tabards, wielding lasrifles and ornamental blades, were pouring out of the troop hatches and running forwards to secure the slowly opening gate. Following them from each transport came an Imperial Fist.

An Excoriator, a Crimson Fist, a Black Templar and a Fist Exemplar.

Or as Koorland knew them: Hemisphere, Absolution, Eternity and Daylight.

They were each proud of their own heritage, of the distinctions that had arisen between them and their brothers over a thousand years. But it was a learned pride. It had been inculcated into them since their rebirth, nurtured by ritual and rote. Now they had been called home, brothers again, and that meant something deeper than words. Each of them wore the brilliant yellow of the Imperial Fists and carried the black fist on their pauldron. Eternity had devoted the full left half of his breastplate to a particularly prominent example and scraps of yellow cerecloth fluttered from the hilt of his longsword.

They fell in behind Koorland, armed, intense, each the very best that a human being could become, and together five proud sons of Dorn marched on the Great Chamber.

The Senatorum was in recess.

Lesser lords in military dress and civilian frippery mingled in an anteroom around refectory tables laden with canapés, sipping on recaff and talking in hushed tones about the prior session's business. The air trilled with privilege and the clink of glassware. Servitor cherubs hovered under a fresco of the Emperor delivering the Imperial Creed, weaving between columns and vid-capture drones bearing reams of parchment. A steady stream of dignitaries hurried from the ablutorials, hands still wet, and made for the waiting doors to the Great Chamber. A polite chime sounded through the vox-casters set up in the vaults, sounding the recall to session.

It all stopped as Koorland and the Last Wall strode past.

The Space Marines towered over the human lords like god-kings out of legend. A few hundred Lucifer Blacks, officers of the Adeptus Arbites and Palace Defence Forces, as well as liveried attachés of the High Lords, watched from various discreet corner rooms and side corridors, but stood off. Whether out of fear of his brothers or hesitation over stepping on another's jurisdiction, Koorland could not care.

He turned to face the doors.

They were vast, oak, inlaid and fretted with silver from

which an energy-nullifying protection field hummed. They were also open. Koorland focused his hearing on what lay beyond. His Lyman's ear cued him to the strains of Ecclesiarch Mesring delivering the commencement blessing.

'*Bestia, qui in sapientia.*'

As the Adeptus Astartes' adherence to the secular Imperial Truth minimised direct contact with the Ecclesiarchy, he knew little of the forms and practices.

'*Benedicat serviamus in regens et nos iterum.*'

But even to him, the Ecclesiarch's address sounded strange.

'*Ave Veridus est.*'

There was no time to dwell on it further as the Space Marines passed through the open doors and into the Great Chamber.

The tiered auditorium was almost empty. Row upon row of flipped-back wooden pews surrounded the central dais and a woolly throng of minor dignitaries milling around their seats. As Koorland was expecting, Ecclesiarch Mesring had the podium. There was an unkemptness to his hair and dress and an almost feral fervour in his eyes as he spoke, his voice coming asynchronously from the vox-casters positioned around the chamber.

Lord Admiral Lansung and Fabricator General Kubik were the only two presently seated, the pair sniping at one another across the intervening chairs. The others moved around the main platform, stretching their legs and taking sips of purified water, half-listening to the aides, analysts and codifiers that pursued them around the base of the dais.

It was Lansung who saw Koorland first.

His face blanched as Hemisphere and Absolution spread out around the standing galleries on the outer edge of the chamber and swung their bolters to cover the dais. As well he might – the fat fool's politicking had done more to end the Imperial Fists than any ork or Chrome. People began to cry out and went to ground amongst the pews. Daylight and Eternity hung back, spear and sword raised respectively, as Koorland marched down the aisle.

A huge statue of Rogal Dorn stood to one side. He faced the aisle, the personal guarantor of safety to all delegates to this chamber, but his gaze was turned towards the dais, ever in judgement of the successors to his god-like brothers and father.

There, Koorland stopped.

There were other doors into the Great Chamber, other aisles to the dais, but Koorland had studied his battlefield and knew what terrain it had to exploit. His armour shone bright and perfect under the lighting directed onto the statue, and the impact of standing so outfitted before his own primarch, he who was the very symbol of this chamber's endurance, was wholly deliberate.

Udin Macht Udo pulled the Ecclesiarch from the podium. He took the lectern bar in both hands and glared into the stage lights over the fan array of vox-pickups. His braided grand admiral's uniform was luminous white and glittered with medals, power and pomposity in bald measure. His scarred face was pink and furious, his maimed eye gleaming like a pearl in oyster flesh.

'This assembly has heard your petition, Koorland, and dismissed it. We legislated the immediate dispersal of your *Last*

Wall to their Chapters. Is this your idea of a coup? Will the Imperial Fists forever be remembered for the failed over-throw of the government of Holy Terra?'

Koorland took a moment to centre himself and to allow the lords to clamour down.

Instinctually, he scanned the chamber for Vangorich, an ally, but if the Grand Master was present at all then he was hidden amongst the lesser lords. His battleplate sensors called back no hostile targets. Another reason to prefer the battlefield. The words of Roboute Guilliman came to his mind then, written an age ago, at a time when such a future seemed possible for the then Legiones Astartes.

'*Space Marines would excel in peace as they excel in war, for the Emperor has crafted them to excel.*'

And more even than that: he was an Imperial Fist stand-ing his ground.

'My duty is to the defence of Terra, and the persecution of the enemies of Man.' Koorland did not need a vox-caster array. He did not shout, but his voice, engineered for the infinite warzones of the stars, boomed to every corner of the auditorium. 'You call yourselves a government, but right now, Udo, what I see before me are enemies of Man.'

The High Lords' protestations of shock and outrage served only to emphasise the schism between them. The impos-ing Provost-Marshal Vernor Zeck was nodding along with Koorland's words, and sharing a glance with the equally thoughtful Inquisitorial Representatives. On the opposite side of the divide, Mesring cried murder, apostasy and worse. The Lord Commander bared his teeth and laughed.

'You should have brought more men.'

'Daylight,' Koorland called. 'What was your personal tally of kills from the siege of Eidolica?'

'Nine hundred and eight of the greenskins, brother. A long night fought over the promethium flats of my home, and then when the sun rose and my armour burned and my bolter ran dry and my chainsword died, I killed with my fists alone as the orks sought to take the caves of the Great Basin from me.' He turned to look at Eternity. 'I would have killed nine hundred and eight more to hold it had my brothers' Thunderhawks not retrieved me.'

'Eternity. Your count from Aspiria.'

'Thirty.' The Black Templar turned the hawk-like beak of his helm towards his Fists Exemplar brother. 'Though I was disadvantaged by the orks sending only their best to take my vessel. I had minutes rather than days, and nothing but my gladius with which to do it.'

Koorland smiled. Daylight's rough chuckle filled the brothers' private channel.

'I command the might of the Imperium itself,' snapped Udo.

'Perhaps it is too grand a task, for one mortal to govern in regency of the Emperor of Man.' Koorland selected his words as he would select targets, and from the impotent flush that came over the Lord Commander, he could see they had found their mark. Even Udin Macht Udo could not attempt to deny the truth of them. 'By genetic birthright, and for the Imperium of Man that He built, I claim the title of Lord Commander. Stand aside, Udo, that you may serve Him without further impeachment of your honour.'

Udo sneered.

'I will back the Angels of the Adeptus Astartes,' growled Zeck, almost reverently, and Koorland was thankful that the Provost-Marshal had chosen this day to end his exile from the Senatorum. 'If you can restore order to our streets and sanity to this...' his voice trailed off, contempt showing through the symphonic grate of his augmetised throat, '*assembly*, then you will have my support.'

'And we,' said Veritus. The Inquisitorial Representative clumped across the dais in cream-coloured power armour to take his stand beside Zeck. The two lords were giants – to Koorland's eyes, in more ways than one. 'As once we rallied behind your Father in Terra's darkest hour, we will follow you now.'

With Wienand joining her co-representative, the High Lords slowly, hesitantly, shuffled themselves.

The Paternoval Envoy, Gibran, was the first to go to Zeck's side, then Sark, Anwar and Lord Militant Verreault. Lansung hauled his bulk out of his chair and, with an almost apologetic look to the pulpit, joined them. Even Juskina Tull seemed to snap out of whatever fugue state she had been occupying to join the drift. Tobris Ekharth wilted under Udo's stare, moving like a man with a powering conversion beam trained on his shoulder blades, but with a smile growing lighter with every step he took.

Only Mesring and Kubik remained. The former looked on as though the goings-on of his peers were beneath him. The latter might have had his consciousness diverted to some other host for the duration of the recess for all the reaction he gave.

With a defiant growl, the Lord Commander gestured to

the detachment of Lucifer Blacks that were just then entering through the north precept. They moved in, shock-glaives powered, but faltered at the sight of Eternity, his two-handed sword as long as they were tall.

More Guardsmen filed in from the east behind Koorland, blades lowered threateningly, bands of light striating the enamelled black of their armour.

'Remove this *man*'s weapons and escort him from my chamber,' snapped Udo.

The ranking Lucifer Black, an angle-drawn lieutenant with a soft beret cap in lieu of a helmet, walked towards Koorland. He pursed his lips, his toughened stare sliding off Koorland's pauldron plate to the High Lords and back again. He threw a salute and then dropped to one knee with head bowed across his chainsword. There was a yellow ribbon knotted around the hilt.

'It's my honour to serve you, Lord Commander.'

Udo was boiling, good eye bulging, but he had nothing left to say.

'You are a powerful man by your own reckoning, Udo,' said Koorland. 'But to my brothers and I, you are just a man. Stand down. You are done.'

'I made this council. Lansung? Mesring? I *made* them.'

'Provost-Marshal,' snapped Koorland. 'Please remove the former Lord Commander.'

With a crack of servo-muscular knuckles and a grin of steel, Zeck stalked forward. Udo drew himself up as if meaning to stare the cyborgised Provost-Marshal down, as he had so many others in his years of rise and rise. Then at the very last, he appeared to wither inside of his plush white admiralty jacket, in his deflation visibly shrinking by half an inch. He dropped his head. Zeck's augmetised hand clamped over his shoulder, and aside from a whimper of pain he didn't make another sound as the Provost-Marshal led him from the dais and into the arms of the waiting enforcers.

Koorland held his sword aloft and shouted, cheers beginning to spread through the Great Chamber and into the antechamber beyond as the reality of what the lords had just witnessed or heard sank in.

'The next time an ork sets foot in this chamber, it will be met by the Last Wall!'

The chamber buzzed with new excitement. Koorland's twin hearts were thumping.

The fightback began now.

NINETEEN

Prax – Princus Praxa

The locomotive rattled along the damaged track, steadily slowing as it curved towards Princus Praxa.

The ork pressed up against the inside of the carriage window squeaked slowly down until Zerberyn arrested it with a firm hand to the back of its neck. A buckled sleeper jarred the carriage and touched acid to the raw tendons in his arm. These orks had been allowed to grow large, as great perhaps as those fought by the primarchs on Ullanor, and the continual buffeting made it feel heavier. With a grunt, he drew the brute back into place just as an ork sentry post flashed across the window.

Scrap metal, painted red. Belt-fed combi-weapons in huge, gauntleted hands. Then columns, bullet-chewed ferrocrete blinking past as the locomotive passed under the terminus' flat roof. Sunlight receded, replaced by spotty lumens and the drum fires scattered over the platforms and access ramps.

Gangs of gretchin and the occasional leather-clad ork

were busily loading and unloading. Zerberyn expected to see human slaves performing the greenskins' labour, but what few humans he saw were in chained lines being fed out of dusty locomotives and into corrals. Moving in the opposite direction were big industrial storage drums, light weaponry and vehicles, and agricultural machinery. Orks in rugged yellow battlesuits showing off sneering moon glyphs oversaw the import and export with a brutish efficiency that any crude hierarchy would recognise. In another setting, Zerberyn might have been watching Administratum troopers extorting a local militia. Some kind of lumpen, enamelled currency changed hands.

The march of columns slowed as the locomotive squealed towards an empty platform.

A ten-strong mob of orks in thick red bodyplate followed the engine in, streaming down a frozen escalator from a pedestrian flyover. Some kind of boss, broader than the rest by half a metre and as dark as a Predator's treads, waved a clenched fist for them to spread out and they did. At a barked command, two pairs clattered forwards to cover each of the carriage doors. Half of the mob hung back on overwatch.

It was organised. Professional. Not at all like orks.

Zerberyn drew his bolt pistol carefully. Columba and the rest of Veteran Squad Anatoq prepared themselves, keeping hold of the orks they hid behind with elbows, shoulders, whatever was practical.

The Tempestus Scions crammed into the vestibule and underseat areas out of sight, calmly activated their weapons' visual augmenter beams, flexing fingers, rolling shoulders, working space enough for each man to move when the moment came. The rising hum of hot-shot packs resonated through the carriage's metal fittings. Major Bryce angled up the reflective edge of his slate monitorum to the window and grimaced.

'Bloody Axes,' he hissed. 'That's what we call them, for the symbol on their armour. Always kill them first.'

'Noted,' said Zerberyn, disengaging his bolt pistol from its mag-holster.

The locomotive heaved onto its brakes and then cried shrilly to a halt. The Bloody Axes came running in, two by two. Zerberyn checked the countdown timer he had programmed into his helm display. It was locked on *00:00* and had been for half a second.

'Brother Donbuss, are you sure that the greenskin munitions you recovered were–'

A second sun rose over the pasture desert, white and furious, light burning up the track like a runaway train. Bryce grunted and slid back under the window, but Zerberyn's auto-senses protectively filmed over a split second ahead of time. He saw the orks on the platform turn in surprise towards the thermonuclear explosion on the horizon, then clutch their eyes and stagger out of their ordered overwatch formation.

'Now!'

Zerberyn yanked the release cord.

The doors shuddered apart, far enough for him to force his right arm through to the pauldron and open fire. A single mass-reactive explosion ripped the shoulder from a bellowing Bloody Axe. He tracked left, fired again as its fellow brought up its gun blind, and dropped it with a spitting rupture in its chest.

At the same time, Scions in full omnishield glare protection popped the roof escape hatches, swinging up plasma weaponry and hot-shot volleyguns and raking the platform with fire.

Zerberyn got his fingers between his pauldron plate and the doors and pushed them open. He jumped two-footed onto the platform, cracking into it. A Bloody Axe flailed for him with eyes closed. A headshot exploded it, just as the window behind him shattered.

Arriving at his own decision to move now rather than wait for his captain, Columba simply fired through the window on full-auto. Propellant trails criss-crossed the platform. Mass-reactive kill-shots painted it red. With their lighter profiles, the Scions climbed easily though the broken frames. Bryce was first onto the platform, emptying a charge cell into the Bloody Axe boss' body armour, and then scrambling behind a pillar as the blinded ork let rip with a racketing burst of fire.

Kalkator executed the creature with a single bolt-round between the shoulder blades.

The warsmith stood on the platform by the doors of the rear carriage. He threw a mock salute. The orks at that end of the platform were dead. Traitor Space Marines were disembarking to take up firing positions over the shredded remains while, in a gnarl of corrupted motors, the three Terminators formed up into a line, *a wall*, and advanced on the steps up to the flyover. The escalator was a natural choke point and, drawn by the gunfire, orks were already piling bodies and heavy guns up behind the bent crush barrier at the top.

Tactical Dreadnought plate had been built to withstand the worst a hostile galaxy could give out.

It withstood this.

'Major,' Zerberyn boomed over the screams and thunder of abused plasteel. 'Do you know where my cousin is leading us?'

'Yes, lord – streetside access.'

Zerberyn looked around quickly. The station was a maze of platforms, overpasses and panting locomotives that echoed with bestial shouts and weapons flare. Engines thundered through, not frequently, but at a speed and irregularity that made the tracks a genuine hazard, even for a Space Marine.

'Do you know an alternate route?'

'I do, lord.'

'Then take it. We will force the direct route. Columba, take a five-man combat squad, go with him.'

With a metallic growl, the veteran-sergeant jumped into the tracks in the direction that Bryce and the Tempestus Scions were moving. Donbuss, Borhune, Nalis and Tarsus fell in with him, squeezing off controlled bursts at the orks on the far side whenever the locomotives screeching between them left space for a shot. Zerberyn turned to the Iron Warriors.

The Terminators walked into a gauntlet of missiles, bombs and explosive rounds like a vehicle's dozer blade churning up a minefield. Kalkator and the Traitor Space Marines moved up behind them, taking snapshots over the massive head and shoulder armour of their Cataphractii brothers.

Zerberyn accorded their efficiency a grudging admiration.

Goaded beyond their febrile discipline, the orks poured over the crush barriers with a roar. Bodies exploded, ripped apart by mass-reactive rounds. The muzzle flashes of rapid-firing combi-bolters strobed in the narrow space. Beasts howled. Piped laughter boomed from helmet speakers.

Tough alien flesh met ceramite composite like knuckles flying into a riot shield. Against men, against lesser orks, the line of Terminators would have been enough, but since the death of Eidolica, Zerberyn had never seen orks like these.

A brute in black-and-white bodyplate, almost of a size with the Terminators, hammered its axe into the lead warrior's gorget protector and bulled him aside. It roared, axe stuck in the Terminator, heaved a Traitor Space Marine up over its head and hurled him off the stair. It took a combat knife under its armpit, grunted, and elbowed the Iron Warrior so hard his plastron buckled under it. Then, severed fibre bundles sputtering with his armour spirit's fury, the Terminator came about and pulped the rampaging ork with the crackling discharge from his power fist.

But the line had already given.

Zerberyn killed two orks with two shots. Neat. Perfect. A third he demolished with a hammer blow. Tosque and Reoch closed in alongside. Too close for bolter work, the veteran-brothers made a wall of their knives.

'Break them,' barked Kalkator. His chainsword chewed messily through an ork's leg while the full-sized bolter held steady in his bionic grip kicked out bursts of semi-automatic fire into the pack. 'Would you have our cousins think us weak?'

Growling their rancour, the Terminators slammed back

into line and pushed on with visceral determination. In a blizzard of bolter fire they took the crush barrier. Traitor Space Marines spread out onto the walled flyover in both directions and immediately started firing.

'Brother Karva, rearguard,' said Zerberyn.

Restricted in the use of his heavy flamer by the close fighting, Karva had held back on the platform until then. Antille came up with him, firing from the chest.

'Agreed, brother-captain.'

'Cataphractii forward. Brothers to the flanks. Grind them under your heels.'

'Iron within!' blurted a heavily augmented warrior of the Chosen.

'Iron without!' came the return, and a shiver ran down Zerberyn's spine.

They started forwards, like a phalanx from the Age of Bronze re-enacted from a treatise on ancient tactica. Shields forward, shields side, spears up, advancing as one.

As Guilliman had once written: man never changes, so war never changes.

Cutting themselves a path with bolter and power fist, the Iron Warriors and Fists Exemplar ground through the walkway and spilled out onto a pillared concourse of polished stone. A painted fresco showing the IV Legion liberating a verdant world lit the ceiling with vivid metallics. Engaged columns, rounded in the classical High Crusade style and carved in the likeness of unhelmed Legiones Astartes, looked in from the walls. A huge baroque timepiece hung from the ceiling's central vault. It was broken, too badly shot up even to make out the time of death.

Orks were pouring in through the large streetside doors ahead, as well as from subway accesses and smashed-up refectory rooms to either side. The space was too open for the Space Marines to take them as they had before and so they charged for the doors, firing from the hip as they ran. Sluggers and bolters chewed old stone pillars to the bone and blasted them apart.

Zerberyn and Kalkator moved together into a storm of lead so intense it was like pushing against a falling wall. Where one was forced to let up to slam a clip into his bolter, the other emptied his to cover him. Where one engaged with thunder hammer or chainsword, the other was there at his side.

It was as the Iron Warrior had said: together, they were invincible.

Zerberyn cleared the doors with a thunderstrike of his hammer and chased Kalkator into the street, pistol tracking like a restless auto-targeter.

The grand old buildings were grizzled by gunfire, their ornate blackwork twisted, pierced and scarred. The road, wide enough in this world's heyday for a squadron of Leman Russ tanks, was filled with vehicle wrecks and blockaded at either end with garishly painted trucks and stacks of burning tyres. A fine red rain fell, gelid and horrible. He had expected it to be warm, but it wasn't. He looked up. Blood vapour and chemicals pumped from the city's rendering plants hazed high above street level, obscuring the chimneys and the higher rooftops. Over the rumble of running engines, he could hear a frenzied, guttural chant. He focused his Lyman's ear, cutting away the immediacy of combat.

He had heard it before, splitting the skies of Eidolica like thunder.

The Beast.

It was everywhere, booming through some kind of public address system rigged up all over the surrounding streets. Another transmitted recording no doubt, but the thought that the ork could be near filled Zerberyn's chest with fury.

'This way, little cousin.'

Hugging the station's columned frontage, Kalkator turned right and kept running. Iron Warriors and Fists Exemplar followed in ones and twos, staccato bursts of bolter fire stippling the walls and barricades.

The warsmith dropped down by the rear of an agricultural sixteen-wheeler that was blocking the way. A mob of orks fired down from its iron roof, laughing, grisly by firelight. Space Marines stepped up and raked the truck in turn.

Heedless of the firefight, Kalkator closed his bionic fingers around the truck's rear bar and strained. The massive vehicle began to tilt. The gunfire abruptly ceased as eight of the transport's wheels were pulled away from the ground. A metallic growl strained through the warsmith's helmet grille as he heaved the truck over and onto its side.

Iron Warriors poured through the breached barricade, laughing bitterly as they gunned down crushed and dazed orks where they lay. Tosque unpinned a frag grenade and rolled it between the wheels of the abutting vehicle. Blast debris blew out around their ankles as the Fists Exemplar followed in. Brother Karva hosed the street with promethium. Zerberyn was the last.

Looking back, he saw scores of ramshackle ork bikes

manoeuvering through the roadblocks at the street's opposite end. From the vandalised tenement habs across the way, portcullis-like sheets of metal were being withdrawn over windows and doorways. Orks roughly jammed ammo feeds into newly uncovered weapon emplacements. Seriously outfitted heavy infantry – Bloody Axes and Leering Moons – and a chugging walker that looked like a Dreadnought rumbled into the street.

Stowing his thunder hammer, Zerberyn crouched by the truck's rear bar and took it in both hands, intending to block the way behind them. The ligaments rose up on his neck until his entire upper body shook. He let go with a gasp – the vehicle was immovable.

'Karva, Reoch,' he called, the strongest in his command. 'Aid me, brothers.'

A missile screwed over their heads before either of the Space Marines had moved. The warhead's on-board guidance spirit jinked it between wrecks and debris, and then slammed it through the flame-effect front fairing of an ork attack bike. An implosive krak detonation ripped out its fuselage, drew fire back in through its exhaust, and sent what was left of the sidecar rocketing spectacularly into the air.

'Emperor's speed, brother,' voxed Sergeant Columba.

Zerberyn saw the green-lit armoured profiles of Tempestus Scions taking position amongst the ribs and angels of the station's roof. Hot-shot and support weapon fire lashed across the wide road.

'Many thanks,' Zerberyn replied.

'Give them to the major. He will make better use of them.'

'Can you see Kalkator?'

'To my shame.'

'Then cover us until we are clear, then circle back and follow. I will praise you both in person.'

Columba gave a snort and signed off.

The road beyond the barricade was lit with drum fires, stripped-down vehicles of sub-human make abandoned around craters in the road. Greenskin dead exhibiting signs of mass-reactive trauma lay splattered and strewn. Zerberyn wiped chilly red condensate from his helm lenses. Drums of the sort he had seen being loaded onto trains bound for the agri-plexes were piled high in pyramidal stacks outside of warehouses. Where those outbound vessels had appeared empty, a handful of these were leaking a gelatinous paste where bolt-rounds had punctured them but not hit sufficient mass to detonate. Intermingled human skins were staked up under glowing electrical heaters. Tanneries. An acidic urine stench infused them and wafting out into the street with every flap and ripple of slow-curing flesh.

The sound of gunning engines dragged him back.

The last of the Iron Warriors were disappearing into an alley. Antille was there, waving for the rest of them to hurry.

Zerberyn slammed his shoulder into the tipped truck, with his brothers' help sending it squealing back into place in the barricade. He backed away, clapping rust from his gauntlets, and shoved Karva and Reoch after their traitor allies.

The alley was narrow and desperately dark, wide enough for an Iron Warriors Terminator, but only just. The walls were crowded with metal escape ladders that vibrated with every bass grunt from the Beast's augmitter network. Blended waste trickled through open sewage channels, carrying nuggets of bone, the occasional finger. Moments before, Zerberyn had thought he had seen the basest point to which human by-product could be rendered. Now, crashing head-long through knotted waste sacks and refuse drums, he was rudely re-educated.

Kalkator's vanguard had just cleared the alley when a pair of spotlights hit them from behind the row of habs. No, not spotlights.

Headlights.

There was a squeal of tyre rubber, a turbo-charged pet-rochem roar, and then an armoured troop truck smashed through the two Traitor Space Marines at point and straight into the wall. The lamps flickered. Masonry pattered over the crowded troop compartment. Orks in thick, spiked armour and enclosed helms fired their guns in the air, the rear wheels still revving up swirls of red dust as the fight-ers piled out into the alley.

Zerberyn kicked in a side door partially hidden behind a pair of bins.

'This way!'

He ran through into what looked like a processing plant or manufactory. Karva followed, the pilot of his heavy flamer flickering blue in the utter dark like a serpent's tongue, then Reoch, Galen and Tosque, and finally Antille, covering the rear with tight bursts of bolter fire.

There were small windows high up in the two long walls, but these had been crudely boarded up and painted over in thick, primary colours. The skylight over the centre of the manufactorum floor had been successively stained red. It was like trying to look out from inside an artery.

The veteran-brothers activated their helm lights.

The beams stabbed up into towering lines of heavy machinery, chopped through steel ladders, and dug into the dark to glint back off meat hooks and ceiling-mounted suspensor platforms. The line was still running, conveyers clattering away unidentifiable chunks of gristle and flesh into the dark.

Surrounded by horror, Zerberyn almost forgot the Iron Warriors.

Firing on full automatic now, the Traitor Space Marines retreated inside. A warrior with a tusked helm and hellishly embellished battleplate tore a frag grenade from a clutch at his belt, leaving the pin behind, and then launched it through the open door. The confined frag blast stormed both ways down the alley and blew scraps of flesh and debris into the manufactorum. At a command from Kalkator, another slammed the door while two of his brothers dragged over a pallet loader laden with drums and jammed it up against the frame.

Zerberyn quickly cast about for another way out.

'We can carry on, further into the complex,' said Kalkator, striding over and clearly reading his intent. One crimson lens on his helm was fractured and flickered crazily, while grey sealant gel welled up from breach points in his battleplate like a fungal infestation. The unpainted ceramite cloaking his apostate colours made him, just for a moment, appear almost noble. 'The bunker's entry point is not far, but we cannot fight every ork in this city to get there.'

'Where is it?'

'And lessen my value to you? I am too old to be a fool, little cousin.'

'Then go,' said Zerberyn, ejecting a spent clip from his pistol and locking home another. Not many left now. They would have to count. 'My brothers and I will hold them here.'

He expected Kalkator to argue. A brother of the Fists Exemplar would have, for it was as deeply in their nature to be martyrs as it was to be contrary. True to his Legion's harsh reputation however, Kalkator accepted the willing sacrifice with a nod of his horned helm and a flicker of his shattered lens.

'Theron,' he growled. The most elaborately armoured of the Terminators turned in answer to his name, in a shiver of razorwire and painful iconography. There was still an axe embedded in his gorget's fibre bundles, restricting his helmet's range of motion. There had been no time to address it. 'You and your brothers will remain. You will follow the Fists Exemplar's orders as though they were mine.'

Zerberyn's eyebrow arched. Honour from an Iron Warrior? He doubted it. More likely, the Cataphractii-pattern suits would simply slow the rest of Kalkator's force down.

'From honour cometh iron!' the warsmith bellowed, backing off and summoning his warriors to follow.

As the last of the Iron Warriors moved past him, Zerberyn brought his bolt pistol to cover the alley side entrance they had left behind. *This is my ground,* it said in his genes' selfish voice, the voice of every Imperial Fist that had ever occupied a fort or defended a hill. *I hold it.* To stop running, to turn and hold: tactical necessity it may have been but that was not why it felt right.

Tosque joined him, then Reoch, Karva, Galen and Antille, pauldron to pauldron to pauldron in an unbroken circle. Corners were weaknesses. The sturdiest redoubts had none.

A scuffling came from the alley, of steel boots and bulky weapons hitting bins. Zerberyn focused his hearing to gauge their numbers, but was immediately distracted by something else. Engines. Vehicles were circling the structure, disgorging troops. Zerberyn could hear them hammering up to the walls.

'Fists Exemplar,' cried Zerberyn, aiming for the door behind the rough barricade. 'The First Wall.'

A rapid beating like that from a crooked fan rotor droned overhead and the circle of Fists Exemplar was suddenly bathed in red light. Zerberyn looked up and squinted into the floodlight shafting in through the skylight. He scowled into the glare, shifting his aim upwards even as the shadows it had disgorged dropped towards the glass.

The orks were coming.

TWENTY

Prax – Princus Praxa

The skylight shattered.

Zerberyn looked up, slowly, torturously, time stretching elastically into glittering stillness as his superhuman perceptions processed the sudden sensory overload. A million bladed reflections of himself looked out in all directions. Floodlights glared white, beaten into slices by the rotating wings of a hovering aircraft. He could hear the thump of its engines, suspended in time as its downwash held it in the air. Shards of glass the thickness of his hand tumbled. He saw it all. The ceiling had not been shattered evenly. Twelve discrete points of impact penetrated it, huge black-armoured bodies punching through the skylight and trailing glass like bullets fired into water. He began to shift his aim upwards, his brain gunning towards full speed.

'–clear!' cried a vox-fragment as glass cascaded over the manufactory floor.

Tosque and Antille pulled into the cover of an overhead crawlway. Galen hit the ground. Still tracking his aim skywards, Zerberyn dropped to his haunches and covered his head with his arms. Glass broke against his battleplate like a thousand blades. The weight of it pushed him down. His ears filled with a crystalline rush, and he could see nothing but fragmented light and edges. He glimpsed Brother Karva. The veteran was bent backwards and backing up, squaring his chest to the onslaught to shield the volatile promethium tanks on his shoulders. Zerberyn could do nothing but yell an unheard warning into his vox-bead as a shard of reinforced glass the size of a Rhino's troop hatch came blade-down through the faceplate of the Space Marine's helm and staked him to the ground.

Zerberyn rolled, glass caltrops disintegrating, just as a pair of armoured boots crunched down where he had been.

It was an ork, three metres tall and almost as broad, clad in moulded black armour of some dense, energy-deflecting ceramic. Its shovel face and clawed hands were painted in black stripes. The metal parts of its multi-barrelled custom shooter had been rubbed in soot. Even its tusks were darkened. It punched the bright red release buckle of the line harness it was wearing, cables whipping up towards the broken ceiling, then levelled its weapon in one brute fist.

Zerberyn did likewise. Too slow.

The ork's upper body vanished in a splatter of green vapour. An Iron Warriors Terminator pumped a torrent of combi-bolter abuse through its remains, turning ponderously as solid rounds spanked off his baroque battleplate.

'Brother-captain. The door.'

With a thunderous crash of spilling drums, the metal door from the alley shoved back the barricade and orks in spiked black-and-white armour pushed through. The lead ork roared, slugger spitting out lead even as it kicked aside a barrel. Zerberyn put a bolt-round between its eyes. Antille and Galen accounted for a further one each. Tosque hosed the entryway with fire, but the orks charged into it, unloading their bulk magazines as they came.

What he would not sacrifice for Karva's heavy flamer right now.

Apothecary Reoch stood by the veteran's remains, his narthecium's sampler deep into his brother's gorget softseals and the progenoid sacs in his throat. Off-hand, he blasted one of the ork drop-troops off its feet with a bolt-round in the gut. It would take a long time for a wound like that to kill an ork. Zerberyn suspected that the Apothecary knew that.

'Exemplars, to your duty!' Zerberyn roared, bolt-pistol executing one bloody headshot at a time. 'We are the wall that stands forever!'

A blast of rubble buried whatever reply he might have received.

An articulated wrecking arm smashed through the street-side wall, the ork dreadnought Zerberyn had seen outside of the terminus station stamping itself a bigger hole. It resembled a uranium waste drum painted with yellow-and-black chevrons. Its other arm was fitted with a screaming buzzsaw, burning promethium dribbling from a dangerously crowded platform of grenade launchers and flamer weaponry. A bestial cry boomed from its speakers as it swung out its wrecker arm to knock in what was left of the wall.

In a growl of engines, a refurbished Salamander command

tank climbed the rubbled wall and slammed onto its gla-
cis suspension on the manufactory floor. Glass splinters
chinked across the floor or simply exploded under its mass.
It growled menacingly, heaving with excess engine power,
hull-mounted heavy bolter grinding about to maximise its
threat angles. Its original dust-bowl camouflage had been
patchily done over in red, a pair of crossed axes painted
onto the side. A troop compartment that should have
housed a full forward command squad of Praxian militia
was filled by a single enormous ork. Its armour was blood
red, massive plates swollen around a gnarled head wired
in to some kind of vox-apparatus.

Zerberyn ejected his clip and slammed in a fresh one containing armour-piercing vengeance rounds.

Kill the Bloody Axes first, Bryce had said.

With an alien roar, the big ork boss took the firing tog-
gle of the Salamander's pintle-mounted storm bolter and
blazed at the Terminators as the vehicle beneath it filled the
air with fumes. The cry was answered by something more
palatable, but just barely.

They *were* human mouths.

Soldiers in what looked like local militia fatigues, with
crossed axes daubed over their flak vests and unit identifiers
branded into their shaven heads, charged over the broken
wall after their tank. Las-fire lashed the rumbling produc-
tion line and by sheer volume forced the Fists Exemplar
into cover. A las-bolt scorched Galen's faceplate and sent
him stumbling behind a conveyer.

Tosque moved protectively in front of his brother, took
aim at the Salamander and, with a furious blast of white

heat, unleashed the single-shot plasma charge of his combi-weapon. The crackling discharge struck under the light tank's armour skirt and shredded its tracks. Links flapping, it slewed off to one side and crashed into a giant steel hopper that fed one part of the conveyer network. The mistreated hopper split up the side and spewed thousands of litres of partially-cleaned bone fragments and flesh scraps over the revving tank.

Reoch growled some choice words of approval. Zerberyn did not register them. In his horror – no, in the white roar of his fury – he had not taken a shot since the arrival of the human troops.

More were running in behind the wreck. Battalion strength. Maybe more. They had no hair, no teeth and their bodies marked with brands and maltreatment. This was humanity's fate. This was why the orks waited for Terra's surrender rather than simply levelling the world as they had Ardamantua, Eidolica, and a thousand others. They did not want another conquest.

They wanted a client race.

A trillion times a trillion, the citizens of the Imperium were numberless beyond count. As individuals they were negligible, to a certain mindset disposable even, but as a whole they were humanity. They were the gene-seed of Holy Terra, where He dwelt in His incorruptible glory.

Unbidden, the image filled his mind of the xenos breaking Eternity Gate, sweeping through the Sanctum Imperialis, and hauling the Emperor from His Golden Throne.

No. *No!*

He would virus-bomb every last world more than a week

from Terra if that was what it took to end this. He would do it personally.

With a wordless snarl he advanced into the las-storm, flipping his pistol's shot selector to rapid fire and mowing armour-piercing rounds through the lightly-armoured troopers. Troopers? Traitors. The outcome was bloody overkill and better than they deserved.

Around him, meanwhile, the orks' pincers closed.

Tosque and Antille stood back-to-back, rocks of rugged grey where reds, yellows and black-and-whites crashed over, and with Exemplar stubbornness refused to give ground. Inhuman voices bellowed. Servos screamed. Bolters were abandoned now in favour of knives and fists.

Reoch pulled Galen to his feet. The latter shook a jam from his bolter, then emptied what was left of the clip into the onrushing horde. The first to reach him went down with a boltgun smashed through the side of its skull, but after that there were too many mobbing in to be sure what was being done to whom.

The battle-brother's rune in Zerberyn's visor display went dark.

Only the Iron Warriors were still firing. The Terminators were mobile firebases, arms outstretched, wrist-mounted combi-bolters kicking out a remorseless torrent of firepower whether there was an ork in front of their tusked helms or not.

A jet of flame flooded over the Terminators, burning promethium lighting the Traitor Space Marines up like devils as the orks' dreadnought stomped towards them.

Beating a gold-armoured ork into the ground with a downwards smash of his hammer, Zerberyn shoulder-crushed through the mob of traitor auxiliaries to peel off three shots into the advancing dreadnought. Mass-reactive rounds splashed across a barrier of rigid blue force an inch above the walker's yellow-and-black plate.

His heart sank.

A void shield. How could something that size generate the power to sustain a void shield?

He was dully aware of the low-calibre hits stinging his armour. System alerts rather than true pain. His adrenal glands were working too hard to let him feel that. His multi-lung had taken over long ago, pumping furiously to purge the acidity from his muscles.

The orks had taken his world from him: he would rather be damned than let the orks take this one too. But, using his battle instinct and survival, he allowed himself to consider that there might be no victory. The orks were too overwhelming, too powerful, their advantages too great even for the Adeptus Astartes to overcome.

A massive fireball rippled over the ruptured skylight.

A burst of fire from a quad-linked heavy bolter cut in from a high angle with a sound like a loose chain being mechanically spun around a crank. The ork's 'copter peeled open and finally exploded, showering the packed melee with metallic debris. The dull grey wedge of a Thunderhawk gunship banked right and over to skirt the fireball, then descended hard towards the skylight with autocannon fire from some neighbouring building lighting its aerofoil.

Zerberyn's vox-bead crackled.

'Leonis, First Captain, piloting *Penitence*. We picked up something you left behind.'

Gold icons blinked into being on Zerberyn's visor display as Sergeant Columba led the charge down the Thunderhawk's troop hatch. The veteran jumped, landing two-footed in a howl of suspensors with his chainsword buried deep into an ork's shoulder and spraying the contents of its chest over his plastron. He pivoted on the spot. A kick delivered on the underside of his boot sent a fighter in black-and-white jags cannoning through two more. Donbuss, Borhune, Nalis and Tarsus thumped down around him, a hail of hellgun fire clearing space for them to work.

Militarum Tempestus Scions pounded along the upper level catwalks, coming down roof access ladders, pumping round after round of hot-shot las into the charging greenskins. Firing on the move with a hellpistol in each hand, Major Bryce took his own advice, cutting through the Bloody Axes and their human line troops. The expression twisting his burned face was wrathful. Zerberyn understood the man all too well.

Brother Donbuss' heavy bolter spoke with fury. Not having witnessed what Zerberyn had a moment before, the veteran-brother identified the most prominent threat and opened up on the dreadnought. The air became thunder. Shell casings showered the ground with gold. The ork walker's void shield rippled and flared, massive force and equally massive counterforce waging full-spectrum warfare across its cylindrical frame. The dreadnought abandoned the Terminators and came about.

It extended its saw arm and, with a sound like a long tube swallowing a grenade, launched a pair of sizzling stick bombs towards Columba's combat squad.

Donbuss took both blasts full in the chest. His plastron held together but crumpled badly, sealant gel and hyper-coagulants mingling in the ruptures. The impact savaged his faceplate, tearing his helm half away. The force lifted him up and slammed him into a machinery stack. The rest of the combat squad were peeled apart and thrown to the ground like toys.

Inarticulate savagery raging from its speakers, the dread-nought stamped about and smashed a Terminator across the manufactorum with a swing of its wrecker arm. The Iron Warrior crashed through the opposite wall. Loosened masonry tumbled in, a pyre licked with promethium flames.

Zerberyn cursed. An ork covered in snake tattoos went down with a headshot. Throat punch. Headbutt. Hammer shock blasted a hole. He strode into it, his armour coated with copper glaze, following his own tracer of automatic fire.

A thick-shouldered ork in Bloody Axe colours shrugged off the bolter fire and ignited the jump pack strapped to its back. It rocketed into the air on an arc of flaming liquid propellant, and landed on a catwalk. The platform juddered under the sudden impact. Tempestus Scions fell away, fir-ing point-blank. The ork laughed it off and set to with its powered axe.

The Scions' wargear was impressive, but it was not power armour. They were good, but they were not Space Marines.

A second ork, and then a third, fired up jump packs to get in amongst the Scions. Bryce's increasingly hoarse orders got lost amongst the screams, the crack of bone and power dis-charge. Several of the armoured troopers broke and risked the four-metre drop to take their chances on the ground.

It was no better.

The surviving Terminators had hurt the dreadnought. It flailed, tangling its arms in chain pulls and surrounding itself with a swinging flock of lift cradles and pallets, crying molten iron. A Terminator stove in the dreadnought's mid-section with a blow from his power fist. Even as he tore the crackling gauntlet free, an ork grappled him from behind. The brute dug its claws into the gorget softseals and hauled back on the Iron Warrior's helmet. Fire sprayed from his gauntlet-mount as he was drawn down and under.

Brother Galen traversed back out of the melee, slumped, riding the juddering conveyer deeper into the manufactory like a corpse into the crematoria. Reoch was crouched over him. His binoptics were a fell green in the fyceline haze, his bolt pistol an unwavering source of white light.

From above, the roar of the Thunderhawk's turbofans momentarily muted the din. Glass fragments and shell casings blew out in ripples, tied to the cycling of its engine fans as it pulled away. A squadron of single-prop biplanes buzzed after it with flak spitting from their painted muzzles.

Zerberyn raised his hammer high, mentally dialling his gorget vox-booster to maximum. Iron Warriors and Fists Exemplar together. They had held long enough.

'Fall back. Everyone. Back to the gunship.'

A feral roar threatened to drown him out, and he looked back to the breached wall. An ork of truly monstrous scale, dark skin powdered with gold, crashed through the breached wall recently vacated by the dreadnought. Its muscular frame was bolted into an electric-shock yellow fighting suit half again Zerberyn's size. Pistons wheezed. Valves

screeched. Black smoke pumped the air. At first glance it
was a typical ork build. Closer inspection, however, revealed
a powered suit of surpassing artisanship. The plates were
glossy and smooth, lines straight, edges perfect. Alternat-
ing power fields surrounded the ork with a sharp ozone
burn. It flexed the arm-width digits of a three-clawed power
fist, auto-loaders churning ammo belts through a massive
ten-barrelled combi-weapon.

'You die. Now.'

Its bastardised Low Gothic was kicked out of its chest,
like air from a dead man's lungs, and Zerberyn was too
stunned to respond.

It had spoken. Orks did not speak.

It started to run, beating aside a steel drum that then
punched straight through a support stanchion and brought
an empty section of crawlway crashing down. Zerberyn ran
to meet it. The ground between them trembled. He drew
back his thunder hammer and roared his hatred.

They clashed like bolt-rounds hitting each other in
mid-air.

Zerberyn's thunder hammer came down on the ork's
thigh brace. The local power field blew out and the metal
squealed under the stress. The ork steam-rollered through
him, snatching him up in its power claw and driving him
through the light metal casing of a machine stack.

With a roar like laughter, the ork dragged him from the
wreckage and swung him about as though he were promethium jelly on the monster's claws.

Even for his transhuman physiology, the g-force was tremendous. Black spots appeared in front of his eyes. He

unloaded his pistol into the ork's upper torso power field until the hammer struck an empty chamber. He had no more. Screaming, he hawked up acid from his Betcher's gland and spat it into the ork's face. Green smoke sizzled from its jaw, but it did not feel it.

The ork tightened its grip. The power fist's disruption field burned off his armour layer by layer. Ceramite creaked, crunched, split. He may have screamed again. He was no longer sure. He lashed out with his thunder hammer.

He did not know what it hit, but it hit something.

The ork bellowed in pain, and the next he knew he was flying with all the power of that immense battlesuit behind him.

He passed through something metal-lined and hollow, hit the ground in a mangle of limbs and bounced once, twice, then skidded. His battleplate tore up sparks from the ferrocrete surface. He slammed up against a wall and flopped down. He saw Reoch, Antille and a number of helmed Scions, but the anonymously-armoured humans swam together.

Then the ten-centimetre-thick plasteel doors that he had just slid though clamped onto his trailing greave.

'Reverse it,' growled Reoch.

'I'm trying!' came Antille's voice.

Zerberyn grunted, willing his mind to stop spinning, and pulled on his trapped leg. It did not move. Dirty smoke was beginning to pour out of the door's pneumatics.

From the other side of the door, there was a bellow of fury. The ground began to shake as something massive took a run-up. Reoch inserted the fierce muzzle of his

Umbra-pattern pistol into the gap between the doors. The Apothecary fired on full-auto, bolt pistol beating against the metal frames like a hammer drill.

The doors continued to try and close.

Zerberyn gave one last roar, then spasmed back to the floor in agony as the heavy plasteel cracked bonded ceramite and armaplas like steel pliers on a nut, and snapped his strengthened tibia roughly in two. His genhanced neurochemistry prevented the pain from disabling him, but it was still as close to intolerable as he had ever known. His conscious brain protectively shut itself down for a moment, his twin hearts racing to pump an endorphin rush of pain-suppressing hormones into his bloodstream.

The doors stalled about half a leg-width apart.

Zerberyn looked up, saw the sheathed chainsword hanging from Major Bryce's hip.

The Scion read his look, unhitching the blade and thumbing the power. Adamantium teeth revved hungrily.

'Forgive me, lord.'

'Hurry up and do it.'

Bryce hacked down. Zerberyn roared as the motored blade ate through armour and flesh and from there into bone. Arterial spray turned his battleplate red. Chipped bone rattled everyone's armour, flying through a pall of bitter ceramite dust. Vibrations tore through his bones. Tears welled up in the Scion's eyes. The dust.

The human lacked the strength to finish it.

With a growl, Reoch pulled the man aside and stamped down on the back of the chainsword, driving it through Zerberyn's leg until it stalled in the ferrocrete.

Zerberyn panted in release. His eyes blurred. His skin tingled with the effects of pain-suppressants. The Apothecary kicked Zerberyn's severed foot out from between the jammed doors. They slammed together, just as something huge bent them out of shape from the other side.

Reoch dropped down beside him and bent immediately to work, using his narthecium's plasma cutter to cauterise the amputation. Zerberyn grunted. His physiology was adjusted to the higher pain threshold now, and he barely felt it.

Brother Antille and the handful of Scions crowded around them. That was all.

'Sergeant Columba, and the others?'

'Through the back wall, following *Penitence*'s locater beacon,' said Antille. 'We were cut off from them, and so intended to follow...' he glanced sideways at Bryce, 'our cousins.'

Zerberyn nodded. He would have come to the same conclusion in his brother's place. It was reassuring.

The door shuddered as something hit it. The discharging power of a disruption field caused it to fold in.

Zerberyn reached for his bolt pistol before remembering that it was empty.

'Faster, Apothecary.'

TWENTY-ONE

Prax – Princus Praxa

Zerberyn limped down the unlit manufactorum hallway, leaning into Brother Antille's shoulder to support himself on his remaining foot. The darkness was near absolute, leavened only by the green beams of the Scions' visual augmenters. It was enough to make out the old blood and las-burns on the walls. The Praxians here had fought. Bestial cries and gunfire echoed through the abandoned rooms. He tried to inject some haste into his stride, but he had yet to adapt to his altered anatomy. A human would have been killed by blood loss or systemic shock by now, but his superiority over human norms was scant consolation.

After several minutes, the rattle of orkish fire growing nearer, the corridor took a ninety-degree turn.

In place of the wall that should have been in front of them, however, was a brick pile. There had been a false wall here. Behind it, illuminated now by the six Scions' targeting beams, was a blast door that clearly had no due place in an agri-processing facility, large enough to admit a Space

Marine in Tactical Dreadnought Armour. It looked like solid adamantium.

And the Iron Warriors had left it locked behind them. Reoch stepped forward and laid his gauntlets on the door. He turned back. His augmeticised face was a glowing skull in the gloom. He shook his head.

Unbreakable.

'What now?' Antille murmured.

Swallowing a curse that he could not afford to let the Scions hear, Zerberyn looked away from the door, manoeuvering himself towards the rune-numeric console mounted just inside the frame. Set into the terminal alongside the keypad was a palm scanner.

Kalkator had said that the base's concealed entrances were secured by a genetic lock. There was genetic variation enough between the IV and their hated cousins of the VII to differentiate them with a fine enough scan, but Kalkator had also said that this fortress was built early in the Great Crusade. And that had been a different time, a time when his gene-ancestors and Kalkator might without rancour have called one another friend and brother.

For long seconds he hesitated, then removed his gauntlet and pushed his palm to the reader.

A red bar backlit the panel and scanned upwards. The light disappeared. Zerberyn tensed. There was a rumble of magnetic seals decoupling and the metal-on-metal scrape of disengaging locks. Zerberyn let out a breath as the blast door slid open.

'From honour cometh iron. Have admittance, son of my brother.'

The voice was a scratchy, ancient recording, but retained some of the power it must once have held in flesh. It was strength, indomitable iron, something that time and worse than time could never fully corrupt. Zerberyn shivered, uncertain whether he had just been given a rare gift or the darkest curse.

'Was that...?'

'To what circle of damnation has he led us?' said Reoch, his voice a whispered, almost reverential growl.

Visual augmenter beams painted the wall behind the blast door with green bands. It was a circular chamber about the same size as the interior of a drop pod, large enough to accommodate twelve Space Marines in full battleplate. Controls blinked in a variety of different colours. Diodes indicated up and down. Only the 'down' was illuminated, a soft white. It was an elevator.

With a nod to Antille, Zerberyn led them in.

Bryce and the Scions flowed in behind him, with Reoch entering last. The Apothecary examined the selector panel. The different levels of the complex were each indicated by an ivory button marked, from top to bottom, with an incrementally decreasing numeral. Reoch shrugged and punched the lowest button.

Zerberyn would have made the same choice.

Exemplars in action and in intent. Exemplars in forethought.

The blast doors whined shut and the elevator plunged into a descent. It was practically freefall. An atmospheric insertion by drop pod could not have been quicker, and the elevator's depth indicators flashed down in a matter of seconds. Deceleration was equally drastic. The Fists Exemplar had been engineered for high-velocity strikes, and even Zerberyn, with pain pulsing from his severed nerves, remained standing. The Scions, however, were thrown to the ground and scattered to the four walls.

Through force of willpower, Bryce managed to crawl out as the doors hissed open, threw up on the panel-steel floor and rolled onto his back. Reoch plucked him from the ground by his webbing. Zerberyn and Antille shuffled out together.

They were on a wall-bracketed companionway at the equatorial line of a vast, spherical chamber. Vermillion alert lights strobed cyclically over the polished steel walls like the daylight terminator of a planet spinning out of control around a harsh red star. He looked down over the handrail. Far, far below, contained within concentric rings of adamantium and brass, was a tank of water so cold that Zerberyn felt moisture crystallising on his face even from where he was stood. Gas bubbled through it, but the water moved strangely, sluggishly.

'Heavy water,' murmured Antille, the acoustics lending themselves to the soft-spoken. 'Used in atomic weaponry.'

Turning up, Zerberyn saw pistons as wide as the legs of a Reaver Titan slide in and out of solid metal jackets with a rhythmic, grinding thunder. Cabling hung from everything like cargo webbing.

'*Three minutes to mark,*' came a dolorous warning from all around.

With Antille a willing crutch, Zerberyn hurried around the companionway to the nearest of several catwalks that projected out over the water tank. He limped down it. Reoch and Bryce followed a short distance behind.

Suspended at the chamber's core was an instrumentation platform of some kind. Banks of cogitators and command compilers filled it, tangling into the descending mess of cables with more wires of their own. There was Kalkator, unarmed, helm mag-locked to his thigh, his face dully illuminated with code projected by the surrounding screens. A pair of Iron Warriors Chosen were there with him, similarly unarmed and occupied with operating their systems. The rest must have been engaged elsewhere in the facility.

'What is this?' said Zerberyn, a gauntlet finger pointed accusingly at Kalkator.

'You know what it is, little cousin.'

'*Two minutes to mark.*'

'Exterminatus...'

Kalkator smiled thinly. 'Nothing so incomplete. Perturabo always believed in complete solutions and he raised his sons in his image.' He indicated the interface in front of him. Lines of unintelligible green code filled the display, surrounded by a mass of coloured wires, switches and dials. There were prominent features, however, that Zerberyn instinctively recognised as a firing sequence. 'Nothing will remain of Prax but an asteroid field.'

'You talk of the absolute destruction of a habitable planet.' Bryce's eyes were wide and unfocused, but the wrath in his voice was tight as a laser. 'There is no graver affront against the Emperor.'

Ignoring the Militarum Tempestus man, Kalkator looked Zerberyn's beaten battleplate up and down. The warsmith noted the way he leaned against his brother, the raspiness of his breaths, and his gaze lingered on the stump of Zerberyn's leg.

'Neither of us wishes for a galaxy in which the greenskins dominate, mankind just one more diminished race cruising the Halo Stars or trapped within their fortresses in the Eye of Terror. Conventional warfare will not defeat this enemy. The orks are too organised, too powerful and too fast. This world could supply billions. Even if we could take it we are too far from reinforcements to hold it. The orks would have an attack moon in orbit in days. You know this. If we are to hurt the orks then we have to hit them *hard*.'

'Chapter Master Thane could request an Exterminatus,' said Zerberyn, shaking his head. 'But even he would not authorise the ultimate sanction on a whim.'

'Authority?' said Kalkator, chalky features twisting in disgust, disappointment. 'I was led to understand that your Chapter was the first of the Imperial Fists' successors, that you carried the blood of visionaries. Your brother Chapters must despise you for your wisdom.'

'Such is our burden.'

'Thane is dead,' Kalkator pressed. 'Magneric is dead. Your founder, Dantalion, is dead. It is the way of the galaxy to renew itself to ever lesser degree and here, now, it is just you and me, cousin.' His hand hovered over the reader. His gauntlets were locked to his hip beside his horned helm. 'I am warsmith of a Grand Company, a rank equivalent to that of Chapter Master. I hold seniority and the larger force. By the principles of your *Codex Astartes*, the decision is mine to make.'

Something inside Zerberyn snapped. He shoved Kalkator back from the command console.

'You quote the Codex to me? You are a traitor, Kalkator.

Legion Excommunicatis. By Guilliman's laws I should kill you now, and then deliver myself to the Inquisition in chains for allowing this travesty to have continued for so long.'

'But you won't. Not yet. Your Imperium needs us. It needs this.'

Zerberyn clenched his fists and forcibly lowered them.

Kalkator was right.

The same infernal logic that had led to the creation of the Last Wall led now to this. It felt inevitable, and no more wrong now than it had been amidst all the good intentions and necessary evils at Phall.

A pained laugh, the bubbling hurt-filled revelation of a man who had just witnessed the dark side of the universe and returned not quite sane, pulled their focus from one another.

Unnoticed, Bryce had slipped away from Reoch and had a hellpistol in each hand. One aimed between Kalkator's eyes. The other at the dented ceramite providing incomplete coverage of Zerberyn's primary heart. There was no indication that he faced down lords of mankind whom he had fought alongside bare moments before. He knew only conviction, the galaxy partitioned clearly into that which fell within the Emperor's light, and all else.

Zerberyn wondered if any Exemplar had ever thought that way.

'Move away from the controls, my lords,' said Bryce. The honorific emerged like a term of disparagement, a placeholder that he had yet to consider an alternative to.

Zerberyn noted the other Tempestus Scions staggering out along the companionway above, groggy but disciplined.

And with no uncertainty whatsoever in their aim. One of the Chosen reached for his mag-locked combi-bolter, but a wave of Bryce's hellpistol across his warsmith's eyes persuaded him to move his hand away.

'Don't fire,' Zerberyn ordered the Iron Warriors, raising his empty hand, and turning back to Bryce.

'*Traitor,* is it? *Your* Imperium, is it?' Bryce laughed again, humourless, and tightened his grip. 'What is an Imperial world filled with the Emperor's subjects to such as you?'

'I am no traitor,' Zerberyn snapped.

Bryce's burnt mouth became a disbelieving sneer.

'*One minute to mark.*'

'I am an Exemplar,' Zerberyn shouted. 'My word is that of Rogal Dorn himself. This is the only way.'

Zerberyn saw the man respond to his words, watched the expression on his face change as he tried to process the complex variables. He saw the expression set. He saw the tension that gripped Bryce's trigger finger, and reacted on instinct.

Zerberyn's gauntlet snapped out faster even than he could think, enclosing Bryce's augmeticised right hand. A slight squeeze crushed the Scion's bionic up to the wrist. Bryce closed his eyes and screamed, dragging his second shot wide of Kalkator's shoulder.

'Please, major–'

The Scion's skull detonated before his eyes, plastering his face in sticky red gore. Half a second later, the arm went slack and slumped in Zerberyn's grip, but he did not think to let go. Stunned, he stared past the headless corpse. Kalkator was there, his bolter up and hot.

'No!'

Hot-shot lashed the command hub with the savagery of truth. Wires were shredded and housings scorched, thousand-year-old cogitator units going up in fountains of sparks. The Chosen stepped past Zerberyn and opened up with a thunderous outpouring of explosive rounds.

'No!' Zerberyn yelled again, louder, caged by red spears and noise.

Antille jerked as though electrocuted. A searing lance angled across his back spun him half around and threw him into an interface that exploded underneath him. The veteran flew back on a nimbus of charge, rolled over the outer rail and, a minute later, splashed into the super-cooled heavy water.

'*Mark.*'

The announcement was a death knell.

'No.'

Kalkator pushed his unarmoured palm to the interface and spoke a command in a language that Zerberyn had never heard. The timbre of the deeply submerged atom engine plunged, felt through longwave vibrations in the gut rather than heard. The grinding sound of deep, mechanical reconfigurations reverberated from the walls of the spherical chamber, amplified by its acoustics so that, standing there at its core, it sounded like being inside a mechanical chronometer as it geared up to strike a long-awaited millennial bell.

The gunfire ceased. Even the Iron Warriors held their bolters close and looked around with unease.

The last surviving Scion took advantage of the lull to

look down over the companionway handrail to the bubbling water below. Zerberyn felt he recognised him– the vox-officer on Bryce's command squad during the agri-plex raid.

Horror dawning, the Scion dropped back, raising a hand to the vox-boost selector behind the cheek-guard of his omnishield. 'Sergeant Jaskólska, Menthis. Evacuate now. Now! Raise the Commissariat and tell them that the Fists Exemplar have–'

A tight burst of bolter fire drowned out the rest.

Kalkator set his bolter down on the terminal as Trooper Menthis' remains splashed across the curved wall. 'I have your gunship on auspex,' he said, as though the past minute had not just consigned billions to execution. 'On an escape vector.' He examined the read-out of a scorched sensorium console. 'And *Guilliman* inbound.'

'Has *Penitence* made contact with the fleet?'

'I do not know. How much do you think the humans heard?'

'I do not know.'

'If word gets out–'

'I *know*.'

Avoiding Kalkator's eye, Zerberyn thumbed the activation switch of what, though arcane in design, looked to be a vox-unit. A garbled overlay of orkoid cant and system noise scratched through. It sounded like voices. Columba. Tarsus. Leonis. Jaskólska. Ghosts, drawn to him through electromagnetic snow.

His brothers would be made to understand that the destruction of Prax had been necessary for the greater good, if they heard it first from him. They shared a singular vision, a rare gift for reason. But Issachar? Quesadra? Bohemond?

The Inquisition?

His hand moved of its own volition, knowing even before he did it what needed to be done. Punching Last Wall protocols into the cryptex key, he hit transmit. Long seconds of alien traffic and accusing voices filled the line.

'What are you doing?' said Reoch. The metallic grille that covered his lower jaw made him look like a muzzled beast.

'What any brother in possession of the same set of facts would have to.'

'Are you sure, brother?'

Zerberyn did not answer.

He was a descendent of Oriax Dantalion: the answer was obvious.

The comm link hissed open, butchered by static, but the direct voice on the other end was recognisably that of an Eidolican serf.

'*Guilliman* receiving. Last Wall codes recognised. Is that truly you, lord captain?'

'It is, and–' He silenced the pickup and turned to Kalkator. 'How long do we have?'

'Five to six hours before it is done. Thirty minutes before we no longer want to be standing on this planet.'

Zerberyn nodded and reactivated the unit. 'And requiring immediate extraction. Repeat, immediate.'

'Understood, lord captain. Thunderhawks are undergoing final flight checks now. I will transmit the pilots your coordinates.'

Eyes locked to Kalkator's unflinching gaze, Zerberyn spoke again into the receiver.

'*Penitence* has been commandeered by local traitor militia. Do not establish contact, and under no circumstances are they to be permitted to board.'

Kalkator nodded. He knew what it meant to betray a brother.

Zerberyn closed his eyes.

'Shoot them down.'

TWENTY-TWO

Prax – orbital

Zerberyn stood at the viewport of *Palimodes'* starboard observation gallery, a hand's width from his own dead-eyed reflection, and forced himself to watch the planet die.

Grey-brown continents and green seas were now wreathed in smoky black. The stratosphere had already burnt off as surface temperatures passed a hundred Celsius and carried on climbing. The thin band of residual atmosphere stuck to the riven crust like tar. A hex-like grid of magmic fractures smouldered through the pall, fault lines, the crust splitting, less a world now than rocky islands floating apart from one another on a molten sea. Bouts of volcanism racked the major continents on which mountains still stood, each an event of epochal destruction rendered into a non-event by the periodic eruptions that ejected billions of tonnes of mantle into orbital space. A glowing cloud shrouded the planet, metals, minerals, voidship fragments, churned by its hundred-thousand-kilometres-per-hour flight and its own increasingly erratic spin. Its nickel-iron core was destabilising. Magnetic distortions caused rocky accretions to blast apart at random, like targets on a practice range, and sent the massive ork container ships caught up in the destruction spiralling between orbits with plasma tails streaming in their wake.

Kalkator had spared no detail of the likely progression. Had he not been as forthcoming, then Zerberyn would have insisted.

The planet-cracker had been fired directly into the planet's mantle through a kilometres-long shaft sunk a thouand years before for this sole purpose. From there the warhead had slowed, drilling through a further thousand kilometres of semi-molten rock to its long-programmed detonation site at the interstitial layer between core and mantle.

Within that narrow variance of pressure and density, it had detonated.

Zerberyn had never devoted much prior thought to the complete destruction of a planetary body, but he could see that it had been enacted with a ruthlessness and a precision of detail the equal of anything that he could have brought to the task. A detonation within the core itself would only have wrecked the world's magnetosphere, rendering it uninhabitable for decades, while at a shallower site in the mantle the resultant tectonic recoil would have been a slap on the wrist compared to what was taking place now.

The boundary layer. It had to be there. And it had taken exactly the thirty minutes that Kalkator had said it would.

The core's greater density reflected the seismic shockwaves back upwards like sunlight hitting an ocean's waves. The effect on the surface was cataclysmic. Tremors had become quakes and quakes upheavals that tore the world asunder, crust and core between them amplifying the seismic waves and rebounding them until the entire globe rang like a bell and the crust was a shattered ruin.

That was what Zerberyn was watching now: the penultimate phase.

He wondered how many souls had been on Prax. Ten billion? A hundred billion? It was the one variable amongst the specifics of time and forces, and it ate at him.

'Back from me, abomination,' he snarled, kicking back with the stump of his leg.

The servile construct screwed back on its single caterpillar track, trailing the measuring tape with which it had been sizing his foot for prosthesis. Its head was a small human skull with a parchment covering of mummified flesh, suspended above a whining motive unit by an articulated metal spine. Its ears were large, encouraged to grow along a cartilage matrix the better to receive spoken commands. Its eyelids had been removed, its mouth stapled shut. It stared at him blankly until Zerberyn, unnerved by the emptiness he saw reflected in its eyes, turned back to the viewport. With half his weight on an iron crutch, he allowed the servitor to return to fuss about his foot as if nothing had transpired.

'My Apothecaries could furnish you with an augmetic far superior to anything your own might have access to,' said Kalkator.

Zerberyn chose not to reply. Bad enough to have been picked up by the traitors' gunships in the first place.

'I will think about it. But not now.'

'Does watching make it better, or worse?'

'It is an act of penance.'

He could feel the warsmith's sneer. It had a vibration all of its own that carried it across the rigorously atmosphere-controlled viewing gallery.

'One day, Kalkator. One day you and I will be called to account for every life we destroyed here today.'

'Not destroyed, little cousin. Sacrificed.'

In absolute silence, a flash of amber light rose up from the planet's core and engulfed it. It happened in a split-second. Zerberyn grunted, eyes narrowing against the sudden, short-lived glare. By the time his vision recovered Prax was gone, a fading red stain on his retinas.

Sacrificed for the Imperium.

He hoped that the reward would be worth it.

TWENTY-THREE

Terra – the Imperial Palace

The vid-recording was grainy and poor, the field dark, the capture soundless. The borders fluctuated, spawning flurries of black snow that intermittently cloaked the figures in central view.

There were two of them. The first was clothed in heavy vestments, the skin grafts and bionic attachments of his face swollen out of proportion and stretched around a curve to fill the round of the visual feed recorder's lens. The second was standing back, visible in profile as she glanced intermittently over her shoulder. She was a woman, slighter than the first figure, robed in Martian red and bodiced with bronze plates, her face masked by filtration tubes and optic sensors. One arm was appended with a bionic brace that twitched with digital manipulators and beam cutters and in the other she handled an arc pistol with uncommon adroitness. She looked tense. Her rebreather apparatus made it impossible to make out her lips, but from the movement of her exposed cheekbones and neck, it was clear that she was saying something. The distended curvature of her companion's mouth opened and closed in response.

Green bars tracked the movement of his lips. Runes flickered, superimposed over the bottom of the screen, as linguistic algorithms struggled and failed to provide a translation.

The front figure turned slightly, a digital black ghost image hanging in the air for several seconds after. He said something more. The woman replied.

'–recording yet?'

Audio as bitty as the image scrunched up from nothing to fill the feed. The laboured in-out rasp of the man's breathing, too close to the pickups, the rhythmic sigh of industrial machine noise.

'I... I think so,' he said, tapping at a console.

The woman drew him back. Their afterimages mingled for a moment, before the uncooperative recording device cleared the bandwidth confusion and showed just two figures once again.

'Grand Master. This is Clementina Yendl of Red Haven, transmitting from Pavonis Hive. With me is Magos Biologis Eldon Urquidex.' She gestured behind her. The figure nodded at his name. 'I regret that this will be my last report. The Mechanicus know where the orks are coming from. They have had a good idea since Ardamantua at the least and probably before that.' She glanced over her shoulder, then turned back, speaking more urgently. 'My attempt to extract the magos and bring this information to you has failed. I can only hope this transmission reaches you before the Mechanicus shut down this section. Urquidex.'

The magos looked up sharply. The fear in his face defied the resolution quality.

'Tell them what you know.'

He stepped forwards, then checked back as a phosphor flash lit up the background image and a loud bang crumpled through the audio.

'They're h–'

Koorland studied the frozen image in the data-slate: the magos looking over his shoulder in horror, the woman blurred in the act of aiming her pistol. He set the slate face down onto the large, figured wooden table, pushing aside the stack that had accumulated there over the course of the morning. Without the slightest change to his grim expression, he glared into the imagined distance.

The Cerebrium overlooked the Palace roofscape from the heights of Widdershins Tower, atmospheric and orbital craft crisscrossing the fortress skyline. Tech-crews hung in cradles from deltaform lifters in the mottled khaki of the Departmento Munitorum, servicing defensive installations that had not experienced proper maintenance since the last great programme of rebuilding instigated by Roboute Guilliman in the aftermath of the Siege. Pot-bellied troop transports shipped in Astra Militarum regiments from Triton, Ganymede, Venus, and from training bases throughout the system. Shining like a lake under sunlight undiminished by any semblance of an ozone barrier, armour units massed in the thousand-hectare rockcrete square of the Fields of Winged Victory. Lastan Neemagiun Veritus, the Inquisitorial Representative, had told him that the Emperor Himself had watched Horus Lupercal's first landing boats come down from this very spot.

Koorland certainly felt something from the ancient Albian oak panelling and book-lined shelves. Power. Responsibility. An almost spiritual bond to his genetic heritage. But he had selected the room as his private study in large part for the view, an instinctual desire to take and hold the high ground.

Drakan Vangorich stood patiently, hands curled over the back of one of the twelve chairs tucked under the table, eyes narrowed against the sunlight streaming through the open shutters.

'How long have you had this recording?' Koorland asked.

'Moments. I brought it to you as soon as I received it, lord.'

'Your expediency is appreciated.'

'I trusted you to do the right thing with it.'

'Is there any more?'

'What I know, you've just seen.'

Koorland clenched his jaw. If the recording had divulged the location of the orks then for the sake of unity he would have contented himself with that, and put the Adeptus Mechanicus' actions down to simple heel-dragging. He would have dealt with them later, content in the knowledge that there might *be* a later. Now, that deal was off.

'Is the Fabricator General still in the Palace?'

'I believe that his personal shuttle departed from Daylight space port with his entourage about,' Vangorich smiled thinly, '*moments* ago.'

Koorland sat back and scooped up another slate. It was one that he had already read and memorised earlier in the day, the sort of detail to which the human High Lords had likely never devoted themselves. He looked through it, thinking, without needing to read it again.

'Some good news?' asked Vangorich.

'Astropath logs from Oort Base. *Alcazar Remembered* translated into the system two hours and fifteen minutes ago, immediately relaying a request to Mars for docking codes and emergency repair. A request that one hour and three minutes ago was granted with a berth cleared for them at Demus Manus port in the orbital ring. You have more than this one operative on Mars, I presume?'

Vangorich hesitated a moment.

'Yes.'

'Then activate them,' said Koorland, tossing the data-slate into the pile. The Adeptus Mechanicus would give up the location of the Beast, one way or the other.

Mars – Pavonis Mons

Urquidex pounded his hands against the keypad and screamed into the receiver. The terminal was dead, remotely powered down. He bashed the keypad like an infant who had lost patience with a screen-locked data-slate and cried out in frustration. They had been so close. He spun around at the sound of a roughly human-sized metallic object hitting the floor, and flinched back against the console.

Clementina Yendl struck the attacking skitarii like a flurry of las.

The robes of her disguise made a whip-like crack with every punch and kick, and five augmented warriors were

already down. Number six dropped, neck twisted around until it snapped, and she leapt over him, sliding her foot between the legs of the unit alpha as he swung a spitting taser goad. A flick of the knee sent the skitarii alpha crashing down. His weapon skittered across the floor. Yendl was already up, hooking the other leg over his shoulder and punching his arm in half at the elbow.

The alpha gave a vox-synth shriek.

With a glance over her shoulder, she ripped off her rebreather mask and took out a charging skitarius with a discus throw. Long braids of greying hair tumbled free. Blood trickled down her face from the mask's intramuscular attachment sites. Her eyes burned with a destructive focus.

A bolt from her arc pistol sent a red-robed skitarius shivering to his knees with blue-white tendrils of electricity coursing through his body. A cyborg soldier ran at her with the stock of his rad-carbine raised like a club. She turned it on the angle of her forearm, took it from him, then spun on her knees and gutted the skitarius with a swipe of her manipulator arm. Bile and battery acid jetted from his midriff in an arc as he was spun aside.

Urquidex had never seen anything like the Assassin in his life.

An entire squad of skitarii vanguard, the techno-elite of Mars, and she had dispatched them in the time it had taken him to turn around. He almost dared to believe that they would make it to her ship and off-world after all. Almost. His mind didn't even have the time to trigger the necessary endorphin release to let him feel it.

A stream of hyper-velocity white phosphor burned up

the space where Yendl was standing. Indiscriminate shot melted through the corridor walls, the floor around her and the ceiling above. One incandescent missile punched through the right side of her chest and shattered the console. Metal and plastek erupted into white fire. Urquidex dropped to the ground, screaming, bringing up his digi-tool to protect his face.

Even to his own ears, his screams were nothing compared to Yendl's.

The wound in her chest sizzled. Molten fat dribbled. She beat madly at the chemical fire and threw herself against the wall, pink smoke billowing from her mouth until her lungs were gone and there were no more screams. She flopped to the ground, eyes horrifically wide, twitching like a tortured fish.

Several seconds of agony later, Clementina Yendl died.

Through optics smeared with flesh vapour, Urquidex watched the immense cyborgised construct that had killed her rumble into view. A Kataphron Destroyer. It grumbled forward on a pair of huge tracks, the amputated head and torso of an armour-plated battle servitor providing the basic neural guidance it needed to move and kill. Its eyes were dull, mindless, its lips sutured into a rictus grimace of unfelt pleasure. The heavy weaponry grafted to the stumps of its arms pivoted from Yendl's smouldering corpse to Urquidex.

The magos narrowed his optic apertures and pleaded with the Omnissiah for a swifter end.

'Not him.'

The Kataphron growled to a halt and from behind it, gliding under a stinging swarm of mechadendrites, came

Artisan Trajectorae Van Auken. As always, Urquidex found himself cowed by the adept without the need for anything so evolved as words or threats. He looked furious, the physical embodiment of machine power. A squad of skitarii vanguard marched in lockstep to his extended stride, red-robed, the arisen shades of the comrades they uncaringly stepped across. Their eyes glowed like coals behind their steel masks.

'You disappoint me, magos,' the artisan trajectorae sneered, his servo-harness adding its own snapping words of contempt. 'You will never know how much.'

From somewhere, Urquidex found the courage to stand.

'The soul is the conscience of sentience.'

'The Tenth Universal Law,' said Van Auken. 'The misinterpretation of the Omnissiah's wisdom is a common failing amongst the Adeptus Biologis, and no excuse for treason against the blessed machine.'

With a brusque flick of a mechadendrite, the artisan trajectorae summoned the skitarii. They surged forward. Two claimed Urquidex by either arm and pinned him back over the still-sputtering console. He could feel the heat against his back, then on his face as an augmeticised hand pushed the side of his head into the plastek.

'The Imperium will be coming,' he hissed through the metallic fingers covering his mouth.

A smile parted the artisan trajectorae's Neanderthal jaw.

'Magos Biologis Eldon Urquidex, the Adeptus Mechanicus sentences you to *servitude imperpetuis*. I will personally ensure that only the very heaviest of armaments be grafted to whatever the metasurgeons deign to leave of you. It would be undesirable for your body to perish too swiftly.'

Urquidex struggled against the augmetised grips that restrained him, screaming for the clemency of white phosphor. Van Auken glided back.

'You have done nothing but accelerate an outcome considered inevitable since the inception of the Grand Experiment. The Imperium will come, and they will not find the legions of Mars unprepared.'

Somehow, Urquidex's struggles freed an arm.

He lashed his digitools across the throat of the skitarius holding his other arm. Blood splashed his rebreather, and for a moment he was free. He spun around, screaming into the vid-recorder as cold hands dragged him away by his robes.

'Ullanor! The Beast arises on Ullanor!'

ABOUT THE AUTHOR

David Guymer is the author of the Gotrek & Felix
novels *Slayer, Kinslayer* and *City of the Damned*,
along with the novella *Thorgrim* and a plethora of
short stories set in the worlds of Warhammer and
Warhammer 40,000. He is a freelance writer and
occasional scientist based in the East Riding, and
was a finalist in the 2014 David Gemmell Legend
Awards for his novel *Headtaker*.